MW01268697

shadow operative

the shadow agency
book one

Christy Barritt

River Heights

chapter
one

NIA ANDERSON ATTEMPTED to open her eyes as a
sense of urgency nagged at her subconscious.

A throbbing headache pounded at her temples, and
something cold and hard pressed beneath her face and
arms.

Not soft and warm like her bed.

Something was wrong.

She forced her eyes open as nausea swirled in her gut.

She was lying on a floor.

She blinked and glanced around.

Where was she? The room around her was
unfamiliar.

Frigid.

Unwelcoming.

She lifted her hand to push a hair out of her eyes
when she noticed the dried red liquid covering her
fingers.

Was that . . . blood?

Her panic surged.

She swallowed a scream.

She did a mental inventory of herself. Other than her throbbing headache, nothing hurt.

The blood wasn't hers . . . she didn't think. Was it possible she was bleeding and didn't know it?

Her gaze went to the white marble floor beneath her. A trail of blood formed a jagged line.

She followed the path with her gaze.

To a set of legs.

Attached to a man.

A man who was sprawled on the floor, probably eight feet away.

Nia forced herself to stand on shaky legs.

As she did, pain stabbed at her head so sharply she bent over double. She grasped her temples as everything blurred around her.

She had to pull herself together. Urgency superseded her confusion.

You can recover from your aches and pains later, she told herself.

Nia forced another step and staggered forward.

She reached the man and peered at his face.

A gasp escaped.

Rob Lesner. She'd met with the businessman for dinner at a restaurant to talk about a contract issue between his company and hers.

And now he appeared to be . . . dead.

Blood oozed from a gaping wound in his chest . . . and a bloody knife lay beside him.

Was this his place?

Who did this to him?

How had she even gotten here?

Nia glanced around the expensive, modern space. At the massive windows comprising the exterior wall of the living room.

The lights of downtown Miami stared back at her.

Her heart thundered in her chest.

She didn't remember coming up here.

The last thing Nia remembered was eating dinner at the restaurant.

There was no reason she should be in this high-rise apartment with Rob right now. The two of them were business acquaintances and nothing more.

What should she do?

She had to find her phone. She reached for the pocket of her black dress. The device was still tucked there.

That brought a small touch of good news in a terrible situation. She'd slipped her credit card into the case and had left her purse in her car during dinner. That parking garage happened to be the same one she parked in for her job as well.

But where was her car now? Still in the lot where she'd left it? Or had she driven here—wherever here was?

Her gaze wandered until she saw a clock.

Three-thirty a.m.

Just then, a sound cut through the air—a manic, almost evil-sounding laughter.

She gasped and stepped back.

Until she realized it was a recording.

No, not a recording. It was . . .

Something lit up in Rob's shirt pocket.

His cell phone, she realized.

Relief swept through her.

Without thinking, she reached for the device. Saw someone named Gage was calling Rob.

At this hour?

She quickly wiped her prints from the phone and put it back in Rob's pocket.

She couldn't just stand here.

Think, Nia. Think.

Calling the police seemed like the most logical thing to do.

But how would she argue her innocence? She couldn't even remember how she'd gotten here.

In fact . . . everything about this made her look guilty.

Her gaze fell on the blood covering her fingers, and her pulse surged again.

The police would think she'd killed Rob.

Her gaze jerked toward the knife.

What if it had her prints on it?

She would never hurt someone, nonetheless, murder them.

But the hole in her memories caused her nerves to ratchet out of control.

She needed to run. To get out of here before someone found her. Before anyone made assumptions.

Nia squeezed her eyes shut . . .

Was that really a good idea?

She didn't know. But she needed to buy herself some time to figure out what had happened.

It was the only choice that made sense.

What if she'd been set up? If someone had killed this man and left her here to take the fall?

She couldn't just sit back and let that happen.

She rushed into the kitchen and washed the blood off her hands and arms. She used paper towels to dry herself.

Then she quickly wiped the sink handle. Stuffed the paper towels into the garbage disposal and ran it. She waited several minutes extra, just to be on the safe side.

She shut the water off with her elbow, careful to leave no prints.

Standing in the kitchen, the reality of the situation hit her again.

Nia pressed her eyes closed.

This was a mistake.

She needed to call the police.

But the Miami PD already didn't like her. She'd dated the chief, and things had ended badly.

Mario Cruz . . . he wasn't a good man. It had taken her entirely too long to see it.

A few of Mario's friends had even harassed her— though they'd never own up to it.

Since then, she hadn't trusted the cops around here. They were on Mario's side, not hers. And they loved nothing more than to humiliate her.

She had to get out of here.

The person who'd done this to Rob . . . he could still be nearby. What if the killer planned on coming back to finish her off also? She'd been passed out. If the killer wanted something from her . . . he could have decided to wait for her to wake up.

As the CEO of a tech brokerage firm, she'd had threats before . . .

A chill washed over her.

Nia couldn't think clearly.

She only knew she needed to hurry.

She walked back to Rob and frowned, fighting nausea as she looked down at him. "I'm sorry. One way or another, I'm going to figure out who did this to you."

Nia rushed to the door. On a whim, she grabbed a baseball cap left on the table and pulled it on over her head. Then she slid on the aviator sunglasses she also found there.

Dragging in a shaky breath, she cracked the door open and searched the hallway.

It was empty.

She had to leave.

Now.

Before the killer returned.

Gage Pearson stretched as he climbed from his rental car and hoisted his bag over his shoulder.

Flight delays had landed him in Miami four hours later than scheduled.

He'd almost gotten a hotel in Atlanta for tonight.

But finally, his flight had departed. Now he was getting to his friend's place in the middle of the night.

He didn't think Rob would mind.

The two knew each other from high school, and they'd remained close since then.

After graduation, Gage had joined the military while Rob had gone on to work in private industry. Eventually, his friend had started his own successful technology business. When Rob had invented Water Splat, a game app, he'd hit it big time.

Meanwhile, Gage had left the military and had been recruited to work for a private security firm.

Gage was curious why his friend had asked him to come. What he'd wanted to talk about that they couldn't discuss over the phone.

Rob's message had been urgent, so Gage had requested permission to take some time off work. Alan Larchmont, Gage's boss, had said it was fine, especially since he was in between assignments with the Shadow Agency.

Gage wound his way from the parking garage and stepped inside the high-rise apartment building. The doorman was distracted helping two intoxicated young women as they stumbled around the lobby.

Perfect.

Gage bypassed the man and headed to the elevator instead.

Rob had given Gage a code to get into his apartment in case he was sleeping when Gage arrived. He'd tried to call his friend when his second flight departed, but Rob didn't answer.

He'd tried to call when he landed as well. Rob still didn't answer.

Gage hoped everything was okay. His friend usually had his phone glued to his ear.

Gage took the elevator to the twelfth floor, walked down the hall, and paused by door 1218.

He punched in the code Rob had given him and opened the door, trying to be quiet in case his friend was asleep.

He paused in the entryway and glanced around.

An amazing view of Miami stared at him. His friend really had done well for himself, all the way down to the marble floor beneath his feet and the ultra-modern furniture decorating the place.

Good for him. Rob deserved all the best. The man would bend over backward to help someone in need, sacrificing his own comfort to do so. Rob and his family had practically adopted Gage when he was a teen, knowing he had a hard home life. Gage was eternally grateful for their kindness.

He wouldn't be the person he was today without them.

Gage took a few more steps, contemplating whether or not to call out hello. Before he could, a new scent hit him.

A coppery odor.

Like blood.

His throat tightened.

Gage dropped his duffel bag near the door.

All his senses told him something was wrong.

"Hello?" he called.

No answer.

He took a few more steps, his spine tightening with every breath.

As he crossed into the living room, he paused.

Just on the other side of the sleek beige leather couch, someone lay on the floor, blood spilled around him.

"Rob . . ." Gage rushed toward his friend.

But he could clearly see Rob was already dead. Gage was too late.

Who would do this? Anger turned his blood into lava as it coursed through his veins.

Was this why Rob had wanted to meet? Because he'd feared for his life and needed Gage's help?

He touched his friend's neck, just to confirm there was no pulse. His body wasn't cold yet. Rob probably hadn't been dead for an hour. Rigor had yet to set in.

If Gage's flight hadn't been delayed . . . maybe his friend wouldn't be dead right now.

His heart pounded in his ears at the thought.

He found a bit of comfort in knowing that Rob's parents were no longer around to mourn their son's death. They'd died in an auto accident three years ago, and he was an only child.

Still . . .

Gage shook his head. He had to stay focused.

The last time he'd talked to Rob had been around six-thirty.

What had happened in the time in between?

Gage rose and glanced around, searching for any clues as to what had happened.

A knife lay beside Rob—an ornate one with a silver handle emblazoned with a wispy, leaf-like pattern. It was definitely unique.

He took a picture of it so he'd remember the details.

His gaze stopped at something gold on the floor just beneath the couch.

A woman's earring.

It was heart-shaped with a smattering of diamond dust.

Did this belong to the killer? Had it been a woman?

Gage knew one thing for certain.

He'd find the person who did this to his friend and make him—or her—pay . . . if it was the last thing that he did.

chapter
two

JUST AS NIA had veered from the elevator toward the stairs, she'd heard the elevator ding in the distance.

Had someone been going to Rob's place?

The police? Had someone heard something and called them?

Would the cops realize Nia had been there, chase her down, and arrest her?

Or was it the killer returning to finish what he'd started?

She rushed down the steps, nearly tripping she moved so quickly. She caught herself on the railing before continuing downward.

Her limbs trembled uncontrollably.

Get a grip, Nia. No one should know you were there.

Except . . .

What if security cameras had captured her image? She'd gotten into this building somehow. Had people seen her come in with Rob?

Another surge of panic washed through her.

What should she do?

She was a CEO, not a killer.

She continued down the steps, nearly falling several times.

Twelve flights later, she reached the first floor.

Nia knew better than to head to the lobby. Instead, she followed a maze of hallways until she reached the back entrance of the posh apartment building. If this place was like the building where she lived, the door would be locked only from the outside.

She pushed on it, and it opened. Relief swept through her.

As she stepped out into the early morning humidity, she sucked in a breath and tried to compose herself. She couldn't appear disheveled. She had to keep her cool in order to not raise suspicion.

Once she was home in her own apartment, *then* she could fall apart. Then she could think this through more. Then she could figure out how to make the situation right.

But right now, all she wanted was to get away.

She forced herself to walk in an even stride across the dark sidewalk.

A street sign on the corner showed she was about four blocks away from her place and six blocks from the restaurant where she'd met Rob last night.

As she passed a trash can, she ditched Rob's hat and sunglasses. She couldn't afford to be caught with them. It was only smart to lose them . . . just in case.

She paused mid-step and glanced around. An eerie feeling crept over her skin. Raised the hair on her arms. Tightened her throat.

Someone was watching her, weren't they?

Was it the person who'd killed Rob?

No one was on the street—no one she could see.

But someone could be hiding in the shadows.

Would they confront her? Finish her off?

Or had someone just been trying to frame her?

Nothing made sense.

The uncertainty muddled her thoughts.

Fear strangled her, tightening her throat until she could hardly breathe.

Maybe she was just being paranoid. But she didn't think so.

She walked more quickly and kept looking over her shoulder.

She saw no one.

But she could feel those eyes on her.

Why couldn't she remember what had happened?

Had she been drugged? Had someone hit her over the head?

She had no idea.

Lucanidae's, the restaurant where she and Rob had eaten, had been full. Uncountable people had seen the two of them together.

Had people seen her say good night to Rob and go her separate way?

Or had they actually left together?

Familiar panic tried to swell in her again.

Finally, Nia spotted her high-rise ahead.

If she went in through the front door, the doorman would see her and be able to testify that she'd just gotten back.

Instead, she hurried around the building to the back entrance.

As she turned off the main street, she glanced around.

Coming back here was risky.

That person watching her . . . if he were to follow her here, she'd be a goner.

Her fingers trembled as she turned to the keypad on the door. She had her own code, but Addison, her neighbor, had once shared her code, remarking that it was also her birthday.

Nia whispered an apology before punching in Addison's code. The door buzzed, and Nia nearly fell inside.

Once the door was closed, her lungs softened a bit.

Maybe she was safe—for a moment, at least.

Still, she didn't want to risk taking the elevator. Instead, she climbed the six flights to her floor.

By the time she got there, her lungs burned. Her head pounded harder. Her panic was barely contained.

She darted to her apartment and tapped in the door code, thankful it didn't require a key.

Just as she slipped inside, an elevator pinged.

Her heart pulsed out of control.

Could it be the killer?

The cops?

The thought of either one terrified her.

Maybe Gage should have called the police right away.

But as an operative with the Shadow Agency, he had skills and resources the police didn't.

Trained in black ops, he knew how to fight. To use weapons. He knew about poisons and toxins.

That was why he wanted to gather his own clues. To do his own investigation.

He'd been trained to be a shadow, to disappear, to blend in.

So that was what he would do.

Soon enough, the police would discover his friend was dead. The local PD would launch their own investigation. That investigation might even lead right back to Gage. He hadn't made his arrival a secret.

He'd handle that when it happened.

When the government had chosen him to be a super soldier, they'd invested a large amount of time and money into his training. It was more than training. There were experiments. Injections. Covert missions.

Scars. So many scars—some not visible to the human eye.

His friends liked to call themselves the Jason Bourne Club.

But Jason Bourne was fiction and members of his team were real. They'd been treated as a commodity, as people whose lives didn't matter.

They might as well have been robots.

Now they all lived with the consequences of what amounted to brainwashing.

A fact that haunted each of them in different ways.

Right now, Gage needed to figure out who had been in Rob's apartment tonight.

He pulled his computer from his bag—he'd also been trained in technology.

It only took Gage a few minutes to hack into the apartment's security server and pull up the video feed from the front door of the lobby.

He scrolled back to six-thirty when he and Rob had last spoken. Then he began to fast-forward and watch people coming and going.

At eleven, he saw Rob step into the building.

A woman was with him. She had her arm around his waist, and Rob's arm was slung over her shoulders. The two looked . . . cozy.

Gage tried to zoom in to get a better look at her face, but the image quality wasn't high enough.

In the video, the doorman barely looked up to say hello to them. He'd been texting someone, and his eyes were glued to his phone.

That meant the man probably couldn't identify the woman either.

Gage glanced at the earring in his palm.

He needed to find that woman . . . because, based on the evidence in front of him, she very well could have been the last person to see Rob alive.

chapter
three

NIA STOOD at the window and stared out at the city streets below.

She was back in her apartment. No one had come to her door. No one had tried to get inside.

The elevator pinging . . . it must have been a coincidence.

Maybe the person she'd felt following her really hadn't been there.

Maybe she was just paranoid.

Her thoughts were too scrambled to make sense of anything.

After fifteen minutes of nothing happening, she'd taken a quick shower then dressed in sweats. She had to get any more blood off her. Any evidence. Any . . . reminders.

Then she'd burned her dress in her fireplace. She *knew* there was blood on it.

Afterward, she cleaned out the ashes and washed them down the garbage disposal along with some bleach.

Then she'd waited. Paced. Thrown up. Paced some more.

At any minute, she expected the police to knock at her door.

But maybe she had more time than she thought. After all, how long would it take someone to discover Rob's body? He worked from home, so he had no coworkers who would miss him. He did have an assistant, Cormac Westerly, and an attorney, Hector Backus.

Maybe she still had several hours before he was found.

Unless the killer was also hunting her. Then she was on borrowed time right now.

Her thoughts continued to race.

If someone had come into Rob's apartment while she was there, why had he killed Rob and left her lying there? Wouldn't the killer be afraid Nia could identify him?

Her head continued to pound.

Nia still wasn't sure what she should do. If it wouldn't look even more suspicious, she'd flee the area. But that would *definitely* make her appear guilty.

So she needed to stay put.

Dear Lord, what have I gotten myself into? She looked up at the dark sky overhead, wishing a face would appear and a voice would give her undisputable guidance on the situation.

But there was nothing.

deleted the images of himself coming into the apartment from the building's server. Once the police found Rob's dead body, no doubt they'd look at this footage. If Gage appeared in the images, he'd be a suspect.

He needed to buy himself some time.

For now, he'd work on enhancing the image of that woman and then run it through his software.

Once he knew who she was . . . he would track her down.

Find out if she'd murdered his friend and why.

He stood and paced to the window, staring out.

She was out there somewhere.

He would find her.

Then Gage would demand answers . . . and make sure she paid.

chapter
four

PANIC CLAWED at Nia as she paused on the dark sidewalk outside her apartment building.

Was the killer close?

No, the killer had the chance to do away with her earlier, and he hadn't.

That must mean he wanted her alive for a reason.

A shock of fear rippled through her.

Had she been imagining things when she thought someone was following her earlier?

She couldn't be sure. Her thoughts were too muddy.

She walked back toward Rob's apartment. When she was across the street from the building, she glanced up.

Her breath caught. Someone was inside Rob's apartment.

She saw movement near his windows.

That *was* his apartment, wasn't it?

She counted the floors to confirm.

It *was* his.

Nia slunk back into the shadows and watched.

The man paced toward the window to peer outside, almost as if he knew Nia was watching.

Her lungs tightened until she could hardly breathe.

She had no idea who that man was. She only knew he was dangerous.

He wore all black, and she couldn't make out his features.

She opened the camera on her phone and zoomed in as much as she could before snapping a picture.

Then she studied it. His face was shadowed.

But the tattoo on his bicep wasn't.

It was large and angular, almost like a saw blade.

Had the killer come back? Maybe he'd left her there passed out. Had left to do something, to wait until she awoke.

Then he planned on torturing her to get information before he killed her.

Had he come to finish her off, but Nia had left before he could?

She didn't know. All she knew was that she needed to get out of here.

Before she stepped away, her phone buzzed.

She glanced at the screen, and a chill swept over her.

It showed a picture of Nia lying with knife in hand beside Rob's dead body.

~

As Gage ran the woman's photo with a recognition program, he forced himself to ignore his friend lying dead behind him.

He couldn't bring Rob back to life, Gage reminded himself. All he could do was find his friend's killer and make sure justice was served.

It didn't take long for him to find a match.

Nia Anderson.

Thirty-two years old. Owner of The Anderson Group, a technology brokerage firm.

Impressive.

Her photo showed she was a beautiful woman, probably of Latino heritage, with dark, curly hair that fell well below her shoulders. She wore a soft-white turtleneck, hoop earrings, and subdued makeup.

Her smile appeared gentle and kind.

This woman was a killer?

It almost seemed doubtful. Yet she was the CEO of a successful company.

Maybe she was the type who'd do anything to get ahead. He'd met people like that before. People who thought only about themselves.

What was her connection with Rob? Was Rob trying to sign a deal with this woman?

What if she'd stolen one of his inventions to claim for her own? The tech business could be brutal—especially when it came to new discoveries that could make millions.

Gage didn't know what was happening.

But he would find out.

He glanced at his friend's body, and his gut clenched. "I'm sorry, Rob. I'm going to make this right. I promise you that."

Then, just as the sun began to peek over the horizon and light the sky, he gathered his things and stepped from the apartment. He'd stash his bag in his rental car.

Then he'd find this Nia Anderson woman and get some answers.

chapter
five

NIA HAD GONE BACK to her apartment, but all she could think about was how things would play out.

Would the person who'd texted her make some egregious request in return for their silence? So far, the stipulations hadn't come through.

But they would.

If she didn't obey, she'd be arrested.

How would Mario make her suffer for this?

Nia felt catatonic as she sat on the couch with her knees pulled to her chest.

She'd worked hard to get to this place in life. For the longest time, she'd even said no to any type of social life unless it involved networking.

Then two years ago, everything had changed when her sister, Sophia, had been diagnosed with ALS. Alan, Sophia's husband, had left her, and she'd been unable to continue her job as an elementary school teacher.

So Nia supported Sophia. She visited her sister once a

week—Sophia lived two hours north and wasn't ready to relocate—and helped with her expenses. Paid for a house-keeper and nurse.

The diagnosis had made Nia realize she could gain the world but lose her soul.

She'd begun to feel like Solomon. Had begun to feel like everything she'd achieved and sacrificed was mean-ingless—things she couldn't take with her when she departed this earth one day.

Those she loved were the most important thing.

So Nia had begun to make some changes.

She'd tried to become the person her parents would be proud of. Not that she'd done anything nefarious before. But she'd been all about work and getting ahead. About having the life she'd never had growing up.

She'd wanted all the finer things. And she'd gotten them.

But once she'd arrived at the top, she'd realized she was unhappier than she'd ever been before.

Success and money didn't buy happiness. It had been a hard lesson to learn.

Just when she thought she was doomed to feel empty for the rest of her life, a friend had invited her to church. She'd noticed how Amelia, her friend, always seemed joyful, even in the hardest of circumstances.

She wanted what Amelia had.

Once Nia started going to church, her whole life had changed.

Even though Amelia had eventually moved away, the changes Nia had made in her life remained.

Nia pressed her eyes closed. *Oh, God, what am I going to do? Why am I in this situation?*

She kept trying to recall what had happened after she left that restaurant.

But she couldn't.

It was as if her memories had been erased.

Then Nia heard the knock at her door.

It was the police, wasn't it? They were coming to arrest her. The killer could have sent them her photo.

Who else would knock on her door at seven-thirty a.m.?

What would she tell the cops? The question tossed back and forth in her mind.

But she still wasn't sure. Should she simply spill the truth and hope they believed her? Or should she try for plausible deniability?

Nausea rose in her. She couldn't do this.

But she feared if she didn't answer, the person on the other side would break the door down.

She pulled herself from the couch and slowly walked toward the door, feeling as if she walked to death row.

Then she pressed her face against the peephole.

A man in casual clothing stood there. He didn't look like a cop.

Could he be a detective? She supposed that made the most sense. But she didn't recognize him.

She might as well get this over with.

After another moment of hesitation, Nia pulled her sweater closer and opened the door.

Gage drew in a breath as the door opened.

Nia Anderson stood on the other side. She looked even more beautiful in person than she did in her photo.

But he'd learned not to be fooled by beauty. He'd met many beautiful women in his line of work—and pretty faces didn't mean anything. Rarely were they a reflection of what was on the inside.

He hated to sound jaded, but it was true. He would just focus on remaining single and unattached. Life was much simpler that way.

On his drive over, he'd come up with his cover story. Now he needed to sell it.

"Ms. Anderson?" he started. "I'm sorry to stop by unannounced—and so early, at that."

"I'm Nia Anderson. I don't know who you are, but I'm not feeling well." She pointed to her pale face and red eyes.

"I'm Gage, a friend of Rob Lesner's."

She blinked, her face growing paler. "Are you?"

"Again, I'm sorry to stop by unannounced like this, but I haven't been able to get up with Rob. I was hoping you might know something."

She still held her sweater tight at her throat as she stared at him. "Why would I know something?"

"Because he told me you saw each other last night."

Her face was now as white as a ghost. "And how did you get my address?"

"I did an internet search, and it popped up. I would have called, but I couldn't find a phone number."

She rubbed her throat. "I understand, but it's not a good time. I'm not feeling well."

She didn't look as if she felt well, but Gage doubted it was because she was sick. Was this all a ruse to cover up the fact she was a cold-hearted killer?

"I just have some questions," he insisted. "I'm not afraid of some germs. The truth is . . . I'm worried about Rob. I'm afraid something is wrong, and I need your help."

"I'm still not sure what I can do."

"I just want to walk through what happened last night. Maybe something you say will help me find him."

Nia stared at him, a skeptical, weary look to her eyes.

Seconds ticked past.

Then she finally nodded. "Okay then. Sure. Let me get ready, and I'll meet you downstairs."

At least it was a start.

Nia Anderson didn't look like a killer.

But that didn't mean that she wasn't.

chapter
six

NIA CLOSED THE DOOR, locked all three locks, and then slid to the floor.

What was happening? Who was that guy? Was he really friends with Rob?

The questions raced through her mind.

Then she remembered the phone call Rob had gotten. The name on the screen had been Gage.

Her lungs loosened slightly.

The man looked nice enough. Dark hair. Barely there beard. Probably six feet tall with muscles hidden beneath his unbuttoned gray shirt with the black tee beneath it.

This whole situation had the potential to get a lot worse before it got better.

Who was she kidding? This wasn't going to get better. There was no scenario where this all worked out and Nia went on with life as normal.

Maybe she should have said no to this guy. But then she'd realized he could know something. Maybe if she asked the right questions, she could figure out who had really killed Rob.

Then she wouldn't look guilty.

Hope stirred inside her.

At least it was *something*. It was better than hiding here cowering in fear.

How should she go about it?

She wasn't sure. She'd have to think this through.

But she would need to be very careful how she proceeded.

Right now, she needed to get ready to meet this Gage guy.

This could be the biggest mistake of her life.

But hiding in her apartment wouldn't get her anywhere.

Nia had to take this situation into her own hands.

Gage waited in the lobby, fully expecting Nia to stand him up.

As he stood there, he glanced around. This building was nice, furnished with the finest fixtures and decorations. The walls were turquoise, the paintings had a Caribbean flair, and the floors were black-and-white-checked.

The exotic look fit Nia—and confirmed she had money. A lot of money.

Had money been her motive for killing Rob? People who had money tended to only want more and more.

Gage's throat tightened.

Just then, Nia stepped off the elevator, stunning in her black pants, plum-colored shirt, and white tennis shoes. Casual yet captivating, he mused.

He forced a friendly smile. "Thanks for coming. You hungry?"

"Not really, but coffee sounds good."

"Yes, it does," he agreed. "Anywhere you'd recommend?"

"I know just the place—and it's in walking distance."

No doubt she'd chosen somewhere close on purpose. Smart woman. Then again, everyone knew Nia Anderson was smart. That was what Gage surmised after reading about her online.

But was she smart enough to murder Rob and get away with it?

They began walking down the sidewalk beside each other. It was February, but the weather in Miami was perfect. Seventy-one degrees with a balmy breeze. The sun peeked from between buildings as it rose to the east. From somewhere in the distance, a Jimmy Buffett song played.

Nia cleared her throat before asking, "So, where are you from, Gage?"

His jaw tightened as it did every time someone asked him something personal. He had his whole story worked out. It was what he did. But sometimes, he wondered what it would be like to tell someone the truth.

"Wichita," he finally answered.

Her eyebrows rose. "And you're just in town visiting?"

"I am, and I've got to say, I like the weather here a lot better than Kansas. How about you?" He stole a glance her way. "You from this area?"

"Originally from Orlando, but at one time in my life I found the nightlife down here more exciting."

"At one time?" Her statement made him curious.

She shrugged. "I had this idea of what life should look like for me to be happy and successful. I was wrong."

The sincerity in her voice surprised him. It wasn't what he had expected of the woman. But there was an authenticity to her words.

They arrived at The Vice, a small hole-in-the-wall place that played Latin music overhead and smelled like coffee and baked goods. They waited until they had ordered their drinks and found a seat near the window before the subject of Rob came up.

"Have you heard from Rob?" Nia stared at him from across the table, her eyes deep pools of questions and concern.

Gage shook his head and glanced at his phone. "I tried him again as I was waiting for you in the lobby, and there's still no answer."

That was the truth. It would be better if Gage called Rob, and if the police could later see the missed phone calls.

"Did you go by his apartment?" Nia studied him, almost as if her future depended on his answer.

Was it his imagination or did her voice sound strained at the question?

"I swung by and knocked, but he didn't answer," Gage told her.

She rubbed her throat. "I see. Well, I'm sorry to hear that."

But was she?

He had so many questions.

He couldn't allow himself to let down his guard.

Because there was a good chance he was staring into the eyes of a killer . . . a very beautiful killer.

chapter
seven

NIA STARED at Gage across the table.

This guy knew more than he was letting on. She just wasn't sure *what* he knew.

He came across as trustworthy.

But was he?

She swallowed hard as the thoughts turned over in her head.

"I appreciate you finding me," she said. "But Rob is truly only a work contact. As much as I'd like to talk to you or someone else about the details of our business association, he's the only one I'm authorized to talk to about most of those details."

"I understand." Gage nodded slowly, thoughtfully. "I only know that Rob said he needed me to come for some reason. When he didn't answer his phone, I assumed he'd gotten distracted."

She quirked an eyebrow. "Distracted?"

"You know, maybe he met someone and went home with her or something."

Her throat tightened, and everything turned to gelatin around her. "Does he do that often?"

Gage shrugged. "No, but there's always a first time."

Why did Nia feel as if Gage was measuring her reaction?

Nia needed now more than ever to keep her cool. She couldn't afford to give anything away.

Because she felt certain that as soon as she did, this guy would pounce.

Their drinks were delivered, a nice distraction from the intensity of the conversation.

But her relief didn't last long.

Because just then Graham Boston, her vice president, called.

She excused herself to answer.

Nia's lungs tightened at their conversation, at the events that were unfolding just as she knew they would. She couldn't avoid reality forever, but the phone call had come more quickly than she'd thought.

She slid her phone back into her pocket and felt Gage studying her again.

"Is everything okay?" he asked quietly, a touch of curiosity in his words.

Nia shook her head. "I'm sorry, Gage. I don't know how to break this to you. But the police . . . they found Rob. He's dead."

~

Gage stared at Nia. Stared at the tremble in her hands. Observed how her gaze darted. How her voice became throaty with emotion.

She was *definitely* hiding something.

But right now, he had to pretend to be clueless.

He braced his hands on the table. "What do you mean *dead*?"

Nia glanced down at her barely touched latte. "There's no easy way to say this. The police believe Rob was murdered last night. I'm so sorry."

Even though Gage already knew that, his heart beat harder.

He still couldn't believe it. Reality hadn't fully sunk in yet. And hearing the words aloud . . . he didn't have to act surprised.

His shock was still real.

Rob had been his best friend, the one person he'd been able to depend on during a tumultuous childhood. Gage's mother had left when he was a toddler, and his dad drank too much. Had kicked Gage out of the house as soon as he graduated.

Gage had been ready to leave. Yet he hadn't been fully equipped. Didn't have a job that paid enough to cover his bills. That was why he'd joined the military.

After enlisting, his background must have triggered something in the system. He'd been plucked out of obscurity for a special program the military was starting.

All the guys participating had similar backgrounds, which basically meant they had no strong family ties.

It was a harsh realization but true.

People with strong, supportive families would have gotten pushback from loved ones. The program would have failed because of it.

He turned back to Nia. "Do they know what happened? Or when? Where?"

Nia shook her head, appearing earnestly perplexed. "I didn't get all the details. All I know is that the police are at Rob's place, and they would like to ask me a few questions."

"Why is that?"

She shrugged. As she did, she waved her hand, hitting her drink.

Liquid spilled over the white tablecloth before she had a chance to snatch the white cup and set it upright.

Gage took his napkin and wiped up the liquid before it spread.

"I'm so clumsy . . ." she murmured.

"It's probably the shock of it all."

"Maybe."

Gage ran a hand over his face and stood. "May I go with you to talk to the police? Please? I . . . I need some answers also."

Nia studied him as she contemplated her response.

"Besides, you don't seem as if you're in any state to navigate these streets by yourself," he continued.

Nia didn't argue with his statement.

Finally, she nodded. "I guess there's no harm that could come from that."

"Thank you." Gage pulled out his wallet and dropped some bills on the table. "My treat."

Nia still looked stiff as she stood, a stoic look in her eyes.

Gage had no idea what the rest of this day would hold.

But he would get the truth from Nia if it was the last thing he did.

chapter
eight

NIA DIDN'T KNOW WHY, but part of her wanted to lose Gage.

She felt as if the man could see clear into her soul.

Or as if he knew the truth about what had happened to Rob.

Even though *she* didn't really know what happened.

She only knew she hadn't killed Rob. She didn't have it in her.

Even though she believed that with all her heart, the smallest niggle of doubt played in her subconscious. What if she'd done something terrible and couldn't remember? Especially if she'd been drugged or under the influence?

She couldn't go to prison. Who would take care of Sophia? Not her parents. They were off traveling the world and doing everything they couldn't do while they'd had kids at home. They rarely even called to check in.

Sophia's husband had divorced her. She had no children.

Only Nia.

While her sister was never a burden, caring for Sophia was a responsibility that constantly pressed on Nia.

As they stepped outside, Gage gently touched Nia's lower back.

A surge of electricity flashed through her, and Nia nearly flinched.

Or maybe she *did* flinch because Gage quickly removed his hand.

"How do we get to his place from here?" He glanced around at the skyscrapers surrounding them. "I'm turned around right now."

Nia sucked in a deep breath to gather herself. Then she glanced at her phone screen, acting as if she didn't know for sure. She had to be careful not to give anything away.

Finally, she said, "Graham gave me his address. It's that way."

As they paused at a crosswalk, Nia felt herself wobble.

How would she get through this?

She wasn't sure she could.

Gage grabbed Nia's elbow, snapping her back to the present.

"You okay?" he murmured, studying her face.

She blinked several times, still trying to gather herself.

An impossible task.

"I guess I'm just in a state of shock. It's not every day

you learn someone you know has been murdered." Nia realized what she said and pressed her lips together. "I'm sorry. That was insensitive. I only knew him as a business associate. He was your friend."

"It's okay—you're grieving and in shock too."

Gratitude rushed through her.

She wanted to not like this guy. But there was something so sincere about his words.

"If you don't mind me asking . . . did your VP say why the police want to talk to you?" Gage narrowed his eyes as he waited for her response.

Her throat tightened. "According to Graham, the police got a call this morning. A neighbor said he heard some strange noises coming from Rob's place last night but no sign of him today, so the cops went to check it out. That's when they found him. An investigator looked at Rob's phone and saw he had a meeting with our company yesterday. I assume they want to ask me questions about that."

"Makes sense."

The light changed, and they hurried across the street.

Nausea gurgled inside her.

How would she get through talking to the police? Even worse—what if Mario was there?

She couldn't face him right now.

What would she tell the cops anyway? How much of the truth?

Nia wasn't sure.

Usually, in her business dealings, she was so sure of

herself. She knew what she wanted and went after it. She was decisive, a trait her employees appreciated.

But right now, nothing felt certain.

And she hated it.

Nia paused across the street from the apartment building and glanced up.

She shivered as she remembered waking up and seeing the blood on her hands. Seeing Rob on the floor with blood pooling around him.

Then she remembered coming back later and seeing that man with a tattoo inside Rob's apartment.

She remembered the picture she'd received. There was more to come. She was sure of it. Whoever had killed Rob was smart and methodical.

He wouldn't stop with just a picture.

More than anything, all she wanted to do was run and hide.

Unfortunately, that wasn't an option.

chapter
nine

NIA DIDN'T SEEM like a killer. Gage wanted to deny that fact, but he couldn't.

Still, he needed to remind himself that the woman was smart and calculated. It was the only way she could have risen to the top of her career as she had. Being soft and passive wouldn't have gotten her there.

But just how far would she go to get what she wanted?

With Rob out of the way, maybe she thought she could somehow keep more money from the project. Gage wasn't sure how that would work.

But beneath Nia's sweet exterior, she could be cunning and cold.

Gage needed to keep that in mind.

What he needed to forget about was how Nia smelled like lilacs and how her skin was as soft as rose petals beneath his fingers.

Gage had seen her glancing at her phone as if she

needed directions to Rob's place. But the action didn't match her steps. She clearly knew where she was going.

She may be brilliant, but she wasn't exactly an actress.

He hoped that would work to his advantage.

"I don't know why I'm so nervous," she murmured beside him as they waited at another crosswalk.

He squeezed her elbow reassuringly. "Anyone in your shoes would be."

So would anyone who'd murdered someone and was about to face the police. Gage kept that thought quiet. Every action and reaction needed to be purposeful.

The light turned, and the walk signal lit up. As they started to cross the street, Nia glanced at her phone. Her face went pale.

What was that about?

Gage tried to peer at her screen, but she had privacy mode on. He couldn't see what was there.

Just as they were about to step back onto the curb by the front doors of Rob's building, a car engine revved nearby.

He looked up in time to see a Mercedes charging right at them.

Nia's heart raced out of control when she looked up and saw the car racing toward them.

Gage grabbed Nia's arms and threw them both onto

the sidewalk. He used his own body to soften her fall so she didn't hit the concrete.

The car swerved at the last second, narrowly missing them before squealing away.

Someone had tried to hit them on purpose.

Why? And was she the target or Gage?

Thank goodness, he was there.

At once, she realized she was still lying on top of him with her head nestled against his chest.

He'd taken the brunt of the fall for her.

She quickly stood, an ache pulsing through her shoulder—despite the fact she'd landed on Gage instead of the pavement. She started to help him up when he hopped to his feet and brushed off his shirt.

"Are you okay?" she rushed.

His gaze narrowed as he stared down the street. "Thankfully, I have good reflexes. What was that about?"

"I wish I knew. But it's a good thing you were with me."

Several people flooded from the apartment building and surrounded them. They must have seen or heard what had almost happened.

Nia and Gage assured everyone they were okay.

Then a man in a suit and two uniformed officers rushed out.

Detective Arnie Duncan.

One of Mario's best friends.

Nia braced herself for the coming conversation.

Detective Duncan paused and stared at her coolly. "Nia . . . long time, no see."

"It's been a couple of years." Her words sounded stiff.

"You okay? Sounded like there was almost an accident out here." His gaze flickered to the street.

"Must have been a distracted driver." Nia's spine tightened even more with every second that passed. "Almost hit us. But we're both fine."

"Did you get the license plate?" Duncan asked.

Nia and Gage both shook their heads. She'd been too distracted by the text she'd just received to even see the car coming. *If you don't do what I tell you, I'll send that picture to the police. More instructions coming.*

"Maybe we can pull some information from the security footage." Duncan turned to Gage and introduced himself.

"I'm Gage Pearson, a friend of Rob's."

Duncan's beady gaze traveled from Gage to Nia and then back to Gage as if trying to figure them out. "The two of you just happened to be with each other this morning?"

"I just got into town late last night," Gage said. "I tried to get in touch with Rob this morning, but I couldn't. So I called Nia. I knew he had a meeting with her last night."

Duncan studied them both another moment before nodding, assumptions already forming in his gaze. "I thought we could meet here instead of going back to the station. My crew is still looking for evidence, and we'll be here a while."

"Of course."

He led them inside.

Duncan was sharp, Nia mused as they hurried past the lobby toward a hallway at the back.

If she wasn't careful, the detective would see right through her.

Just like Gage.

She needed to plan each of her words and actions with precision.

Otherwise, her ex might get his wish and see her totally destroyed.

chapter
ten

GAGE AND NIA had been escorted into a small office that management at the apartment building had let them use.

Gage watched as Detective Duncan questioned Nia.

The two of them seemed to know each other . . . and Nia didn't appear to like the man. She'd grown colder and colder while they were around him.

Duncan didn't seem to be Nia's biggest fan either. His gaze had flickered with distrust and maybe even disdain.

Gage wondered about their history—because there clearly was one. But this wasn't the time to ask.

Nia pushed a hair behind her ear. Her breathing was shallow. Her gaze skittered about the room.

Anyone in her shoes would be uncomfortable.

But they didn't know what Gage knew.

They didn't know that Nia had come into this apartment building last night with Rob.

Gage still needed to figure out how she'd left. He'd quickly perused the security camera feeds, but he hadn't seen her exit the building. Nia could have departed from Rob's place out a back exit.

Which only made her look even more guilty.

But if Nia had been wearing a disguise . . . maybe he wouldn't have noticed her.

Was she that cunning?

If she'd murdered Rob, then the answer was clearly yes.

"So tell me what happened when you saw Rob yesterday." Detective Duncan sat in a padded chair, his full attention on Nia.

Nia laced her fingers together in front of her, her gaze still wobbly. "We had a meeting at the office. He left around two-thirty, I'd say. Our exchange was very pleasant. In fact, the entire board of directors was there."

"And was that the last time you saw him?"

Hesitation marred her features.

Gage held his breath. Was she going to deny it?

More than anything he wanted to come right out and confront her. But in this situation, he didn't feel like that was the right approach.

"Rob actually called me later to see if the two of us could have dinner and talk one-on-one. He thought it would be easier if we could speak without board members around."

The detective raised his eyebrows. "Is that right?"

"Yes . . . I agreed that it was a good idea. There's so much scrutiny you're under at those meetings. Everyone is evaluating what everyone else says. I thought a more relaxed atmosphere could be good also."

"Where did you meet?"

"We met at a restaurant called Lucanidae's. It's on—"

"I'm familiar with the restaurant."

Nia flushed and nodded. "Anyway, we met there at eight. It was purely business, and nothing else. We discussed a contract issue."

"What time did you leave?"

"Around ten or ten-thirty. We said good night, I walked to my car, and I assume he walked to his. We said we'd talk more in the morning."

"That was the last you saw of him?"

She pushed another hair behind her ear. "That's correct."

Aside from the fact he'd seen the video of her walking inside this building with Rob last night, something about the way she said the words didn't ring true to Gage.

What else was she lying about?

Everything else up until that point had added up.

What had happened after dinner? Had the two discovered they had feelings for each other? Had one thing led to another?

Gage's hands fisted. He didn't like the thought of that—simply because his friend wasn't that type. Rob was a serious relationship type of guy. He'd had three serious girlfriends since Gage knew him, one of them being an engagement that had ended poorly. But he wasn't a casual dater.

It was looking more and more like this woman had murdered his friend.

But why?

What kind of evil lurked behind Nia's beautiful features?

That was what he needed to find out.

"What were your thoughts on this contract issue you mentioned?" Duncan crossed his arms as he waited for Nia to answer.

"It's complicated." Nia let out a heavy breath. "We'd already invested money into the new app he'd designed. We had buyers who were interested. But he suddenly wanted to back out. It was weird, really."

"Why did he want to back out?" Duncan asked.

"He just said he'd had a change of heart and had decided he wanted to tweak the app some more before releasing it. I pushed for more information, but he didn't share. The whole conversation had been surprising, to say the least."

Duncan shifted, but his gaze never lost its focus. "What kind of app is this?"

"That's the thing." Nia narrowed her eyes with confusion. "It's a relaxation app. You listen to sounds or watch videos, and it helps lower your heart rate, lulls you to sleep, brings down your stress levels. It's nothing groundbreaking, so to speak. But there is a market for it.

We were going through the process of getting endorsements from some prominent psychologists even."

"That does seem odd he'd want to back out," Duncan said. "Maybe he got a better offer."

Nia shrugged. "Maybe. I know Sigmund O'Neill, another tech broker, really wanted Rob to sign with him."

"How did the evening end?" Duncan asked.

"I told Rob I'd think about what we discussed and that I'd get back with him soon."

Duncan stared at her. "That was it?"

"That was it," Nia confirmed.

Detective Duncan leaned toward her. "Did anything seem to be bothering Mr. Lesner when you spoke? Did he seem agitated? Distracted?"

Nia thought about his question before shaking her head. "Not really. I mean, nothing was bothering him other than the fact he'd changed his mind about a contract that had already been signed."

Had she missed some kind of clue during their conversation?

She didn't know.

Clearly, something had happened between the time they'd met at her office—when Rob had seemed okay with the contract—and the time he'd called her around four to request dinner.

But what could have happened for him to do a one-eighty? Maybe Cormac would know. She needed to track him down.

chapter
eleven

GAGE'S THOUGHTS continued to race.

Was the detective suspicious of Nia? Did Duncan think she was guilty?

Gage wasn't sure. But there was definitely more to her story.

Duncan turned toward him, focusing his efforts on questioning Gage now. "When did you say you arrived in town?"

"Last night." Gage shifted in his molded plastic seat. "Rob called me around four-thirty yesterday afternoon and said he needed to talk—in person. Asked if I could come right away. He said it was urgent, so I flew in from Kansas. I talked to him last at six-thirty, right before the first leg of my flight took off."

Duncan grunted and wrote something else in his notebook. "It sounds as if something was going on with him. Mr. Lesner didn't hint about what that might be?"

Gage shook his head. "He said we'd talk when I got

here. It was 'safer' that way. I arrived around three a.m.—
my flight was late—and tried to call Rob. He didn't
answer. I went to his apartment, knocked on his door.
He didn't answer that either. That's when I remembered
him mentioning a meeting with Nia, so I waited until a
reasonable hour and tracked her down. It was all I knew
to do."

Duncan's gaze flickered to Nia again, and he
frowned.

The man wasn't a fan. But why? What was the
history there?

Maybe Gage would ask her sometime.

But he had bigger worries right now.

"You two are free to go." Detective Duncan closed
his notebook. "But I may have more follow-up questions,
so stay in town."

"Of course." Nia stood. "Anything you need."

Gage doubted she meant that. She was *definitely*
hiding something.

He paused and turned back to Duncan before leaving. "What about surveillance footage here at the apartment building? Did it pick up on anything?"

Detective Duncan shook his head. "No, nothing. In
fact, the footage doesn't even show Rob coming home
last night—and he clearly returned home."

"Bizarre . . ." Gage squinted.

He'd deleted the footage of himself coming in.

But not the footage of Nia and Rob returning to the
apartment building. He'd seen the images himself. So
what had happened to that video?

Had Nia somehow managed to delete it? She was a smart lady and good with tech. She was probably capable of it.

Maybe she was more cunning than Gage gave her credit for.

"I hope you find the guy that did this to him." Gage was certain to say *the guy*, to not let on to the fact he thought a woman was responsible.

There was one thing Gage knew for sure. He'd need to keep Nia close if he wanted to find answers. His gut told him that demanding a confession wouldn't work. She was too stubborn for that.

He would need to be more subtle.

The two of them stepped outside, and he paused. He needed to think of a reason to stay together without being too obvious.

Gage glanced at Nia, trying to remain casual. "What are you doing now? Going to work?"

She let out a heavy, burdened breath. Glanced around. Frowned.

"I don't know. I really don't." She raked a hand through her hair and stared off into the distance. "I have so much on my mind."

"Want to take a walk?" he asked. "We could clear our thoughts. I think it would do us both some good."

Nia studied him a moment, a flash of distrust in her gaze. He couldn't blame her after everything that happened.

He fully expected her to say no.

Instead, after another moment of thought, she

nodded. "Maybe that *is* a good idea. I don't think I should go into the office right now feeling like I do. I *am* the leader of the company, and I need to set the tone. Right now, I just want to fall to pieces."

Her words sounded so sincere that Gage almost believed her.

Almost.

⁓

If you don't do what I tell you, I'll send that picture to the police. More instructions coming.

That was what the text had said, Nia mused as she stood outside Rob's apartment building with Gage after the police interview.

Even though the two of them had talked about taking a walk, her feet felt cemented to the sidewalk.

Was Gage . . . dangerous?

She glanced at him. He didn't have an air about him. His gaze was smart. His reactions quick. Yet he had a certain toughness to his actions.

Part of her wanted to run. But that wasn't an option right now.

Despite the fact that it was humid and hot outside, Nia shivered. "What a nightmare. I still can't believe it."

Gage eyed her a minute. "Me neither. Who could have done this to him? Rob was one of the nicest people I've ever met."

That was the question Nia kept asking herself also. She really had no idea. But she needed to think hard.

Maybe Gage was just the person to help her do that.

"I know Rob had some very innovative ideas. Maybe someone else wanted to take one of those ideas for themselves," she guessed. "You have any theories about who that could have been? Did he ever talk to you about any of his competitors?"

Gage's eyebrows flickered up, almost as if her questions surprised him. "I can't say he's mentioned anyone to me. But you're right. That would be a possibility. I suppose you'd have to ask yourself who has the most to gain by his death. Usually, those things go back to gaining money, love, or power."

Nia shrugged again before shaking her head. "Or maybe . . . maybe the whole thing was random? What if someone broke into his apartment intending on robbing him, only to discover he was home?"

"Maybe, but my impression after talking to the detective is that nothing was stolen from his place. Besides, the average, everyday robber probably doesn't have the skills to erase security footage."

Nia frowned. "Good point. That does seem to take this to the next level, doesn't it?"

Her thoughts remained heavy as she raced through the possibilities of what could be going on.

Gage was right about one thing. The person behind this was clever.

The killer had set Nia up to make it look like she'd done this. He'd erased the security footage. Now this person was threatening her with that photo.

She couldn't put all the pieces together.

She only knew she could see the figurative firing squad ahead and knew she'd be in front of them soon if she didn't find these answers.

She let out a deep breath as someone pulled up to the curb in front of them. In the blink of an eye, the door opened, and a leggy blonde woman rushed out.

Tears streamed down the woman's face as she hurried toward the front door.

Her gaze stopped on Gage.

The next moment, she veered toward him and threw herself into his arms.

Nia gaped.

Who was this woman, and what in the world was going on?

Gage looked equally confused as he awkwardly patted the woman's back.

"I just heard." The woman sobbed into Gage's chest. "I can't believe Rob is dead."

Gage squinted, still appearing stiff and unsure.

Finally, he muttered, "I . . . can't believe it either."

After another moment, the woman untangled her arms from around him. She straightened and pulled a tissue from her pocket to dab her eyes.

When she peered up at Gage, she let out a long puff of air and shook her head. "I'm sorry. You don't know who I am, do you?"

"I'm afraid not." He grimaced apologetically.

"Rob talked about you all the time, and I saw the pictures of you guys together. The ones where you went camping in the Ozarks. He told me some campfire story about you putting his tent on top of his SUV."

Gage's expression loosened. "Guilty as charged."

She sniffed again. "I'm Brittany. Brittany Stevens."

He remained quiet as if trying to place the name.

"Rob's girlfriend," Brittany finally explained.

Gage blinked several times as he stared at the woman. "His girlfriend?"

She tilted her head. "You mean he didn't tell you about me?"

Gage drew in a long breath. "I'm sorry, but I'm afraid he didn't."

At those words, Brittany burst into sobs again and buried herself in Gage's chest.

It appeared to Nia that Rob had some secrets of his own.

chapter
twelve

TENSION STRETCHED across Gage's chest.

Rob had *definitely* never mentioned a girlfriend. Gage would have remembered.

In fact, Rob would have sent Gage pictures if he had a girlfriend, especially one as beautiful as Brittany.

Gage saw the confusion on Nia's face. Saw the lack of outrage and jealousy.

In fact, she almost looked compassionate as she stared at Brittany sobbing against his chest.

Maybe he could rule out the idea that Nia was a jilted lover. That theory hadn't been at the top of his list anyway.

But something more was going on here.

He needed to figure out what.

Even though he'd seen Nia go into his friend's apartment building last night and she made the most sense as the murderer, he needed to get a better sense of the situation.

Brittany looked up at him, tears still flooding from her eyes. "You've got to figure out who did this."

"Me?" He tried to keep the tautness out of his voice. But he halfway expected Brittany to blurt what he did for a living.

"He said you were the best."

More tension imbedded itself in between his shoulders. Exactly how much had Rob told this woman?

Rob was one of the few people who knew what Gage really did for a living.

But his friend knew better than to share that information with other people.

Was that what he'd done? Gage just couldn't see Rob blabbing anything about Gage's background to others.

Still, he'd need to be very careful how he responded to this woman.

He cleared his throat. "I'm not sure exactly what I can do for you. I repair computers for a living."

"Repairing computers or not—I don't care. Rob always spoke so highly of you." Brittany ran a manicured nail beneath her eyes. "You have to help. Please."

Gage remained pensive before asking, "Who do you think may have done this to him? Do you know of any enemies he might have had?"

"Yes," she stated without even blinking. "Darius Miller."

"Who is Darius Miller?" The name didn't sound familiar to Gage.

"My ex-boyfriend. He hated Rob with a vengeance. I think he may have done this."

Gage stored that name away.

Detective Duncan stepped outside and glanced around before his gaze stopped on the crying woman. "You must be Brittany. Thank you for coming."

"Of course," she murmured, her gaze fluttering up to meet the detective's. "I came as soon as you called."

If Gage had to guess, the police had found her contact information in Rob's cell phone, maybe even as one of his frequent calls.

"We need to ask you some questions," Duncan said.

"You can ask me anything if it means finding who did this." Brittany cast one more glance at Gage. "Please, stay in touch with me."

"I don't have your number."

"Let me give it to you then."

Gage pulled out his phone and typed her information there.

Then she lowered her head and walked inside with the detective.

Gage turned to Nia.

He needed to think of the best way to proceed from here.

Was that what this was about? Nia wondered. Had Brittany's ex-boyfriend killed Rob in a fit of jealousy? Could it be that simple?

The theory seemed far-fetched, especially considering everything else she knew.

But it was another idea to explore.

She remembered that text she'd gotten. Would Brittany's ex-boyfriend have sent it?

The pieces just didn't seem to fit. Then again, she needed to know more before she could draw any conclusions.

"What are you thinking?" Gage studied her expression.

"I'm . . . I don't even know what to think." She glanced up at him. "You?"

"This is all crazy," Gage said. "I'm not an investigator. I don't even pretend to be one. But . . . maybe I should track down this guy Brittany mentioned. The police will probably do the same thing because Brittany will most likely give them his name also. Right now, I have a head start. I don't want to interfere with a police investigation, but . . . I want to know who did this."

Her thoughts raced. Gage's idea was excellent . . . but she didn't want to be left out. "It . . . sounds like a plan. I . . . I could go along if you'd like."

"I don't want to put you in danger." His voice held a touch of concern.

Nia glanced down the street where the car had disappeared after nearly hitting them. Danger was already all around her.

But she didn't want to tell Gage that yet.

"I'm no good for the rest of the day," she finally said. "I already texted my assistant that I was taking the day off. There's no need for me to go to the office. I won't get a thing done anyway."

Gage continued to study her face as if trying to figure her out.

Finally, he said, "I don't even know where this guy lives."

Nia was already doing a search on her phone. She found the man quickly. "He owns a club in downtown Miami. It's only about a mile from here."

Gage raised his eyebrows. "Good to know."

"So what do you say?"

He frowned before turning away. Then he raised his hand to flag a taxi coming down the road. "I'd say I would drive, but it will take too long to get to my car. It'll be faster this way."

He ushered Nia inside the cab.

She didn't know exactly what she was doing right now. All she knew was that she had to find the real killer . . . and Gage seemed like a good person to keep close.

Keep your friends close and your enemies closer.

Which category did Gage fall into?

chapter
thirteen

GAGE WASN'T sure he should be bringing Nia with him to question this Darius guy.

On the other hand, he needed to figure out her motive. Needed to find evidence to seal the deal that she was the killer.

But he was curious also about this Darius guy . . . as well as about Brittany.

Why hadn't Rob mentioned Brittany to Gage? It still seemed strange and suspicious within itself.

However, his friend had seemed both anxious and happy lately. A strange combination, but Gage supposed it just depended on which moment he was talking to Rob.

One day, Rob would be talking about the amazing opportunities before him. The next day, he'd sound downcast as he fretted over new ideas and what he wanted to do with them.

He'd had amazing success with Water Splat. He'd

been developing another app for the past several months. The last time Gage had spoken with him, Rob had a third idea he wanted to pursue, one he was really excited about.

He hadn't shared any details with Gage, though.

All he'd said was, "Big decisions. I have big decisions to make."

Gage hadn't asked what exactly that meant. He figured he'd find out when he came here to visit. Now it was too late. Whatever those big ideas were that Rob was working on, Gage might never know.

The cab pulled to a stop in front of Avenue 12, and he and Nia stepped out.

They paused on the sidewalk, and Gage stared at the club's simple black sign with the cursive letters above a set of tinted glass doors. A brute of a man slipped inside, which led Gage to again question whether or not he should have let Nia come with him.

But why should he feel protective of her if she was a killer?

His thoughts collided inside him. He knew they didn't make sense. But they were there, nonetheless.

He and Nia were here, so he'd need to make the most of this situation.

"You ready for this?" he asked Nia quietly.

She stared at the building, trepidation in her gaze. Finally, she nodded. "I am."

They walked to the door, and the brute stepped out. He crossed his arms as he blocked them. As he did, his jacket moved, revealing a gun tucked into a holster near his shoulder.

"We're closed," the man announced.

"I'm hoping to talk to Darius," Gage said. "It's important."

"About what?" the man growled.

"A personal matter."

The bouncer only grunted. "You're going to need to do better than that. Either you have an appointment or you leave."

Nia stepped closer, an easy smile plastered on her face. "I'm wondering if you all are looking for any investors here at Avenue 12. I'm interested. Very interested."

"Who are you?"

"Nia Anderson with The Anderson Group."

The bouncer stared at her a moment before touching something on a headset at his ear and mumbling into it.

Gage tried not to be impressed with Nia. But he was.

Nia had been calm and cool under pressure.

Just like any good killer might be, he supposed. And, for that matter, she was a far better actress than he would have guessed.

The bouncer turned back to them. "He'll see you."

Gage let out his breath.

Nia's excuse had worked. Now they would need to go inside and sell it.

He hoped Nia could do that.

Because he was already getting bad vibes from this place.

Dangerous vibes.

And he hoped he wasn't walking into a trap.

Nia tried to ignore the rumble of nerves sweeping through her as she and Gage stepped inside the club.

The place was dark with red accents and black leather furniture. It smelled like whiskey and expensive cologne —maybe even a touch of Cuban cigars.

This wasn't a club for teens or the poor.

This was a club for the elite.

It wasn't the type of establishment she frequented. Even back when she'd been bent on experiencing all the world had to offer, she'd still had her limits.

And this place—though exquisite and rich—had sleezy undertones.

"You don't have to do this," Gage murmured in her ear as they walked.

"But I do."

"Why in the world do you *need* to do this?"

She didn't answer, and thankfully Gage didn't have time to press.

Good . . . because Nia didn't know what to tell him. If she shared too much, his suspicions might rise. He might not want to work with her to find answers.

The bouncer led them through the dining area and dance floor and around back to where the offices were located.

He opened a door, and they were escorted into a large office. "Mr. Miller . . ."

"Thank you, Cal. Close the door behind you, please."

Darius Miller sat behind a massive desk. The man was large with broad shoulders and a barrel belly. His head had been shaved, but his thick eyebrows more than made up for his baldness. His pinstripe black suit reminded Nia of a mafia kingpin.

"You wanted to see me?" Darius observed Nia with calculating eyes.

A tremble of fear raked through her.

What if she was staring at Rob's killer right now? What if he knew who she was? If he was the one who'd set her up and sent her that text?

Maybe she shouldn't have come here. But it was too late now.

Nia lifted her chin and shifted back into professional mode. She'd stared down competitors. Brokered deals with cold-hearted tycoons. Fought to get ahead in a cut-throat business world.

She introduced herself and her background before going through her spiel about her desire to potentially invest in this place.

She tried to read Darius's gaze as she spoke, tried to see if there was any recognition there.

Nia wasn't sure.

He eyed her with a skeptical gaze, smoke from a cigar hanging in the air. "Who sent you here? Or are you telling me you're just a fan of my club and you decided to stop by uninvited?"

She hesitated a second before saying, "Brittany told me about this place, and it piqued my interest."

His eyebrows shot up. "Brittany? She hates me. Why would she sing the praises of my club like she only wants the best for me or something?"

The look in the man's eyes was cold and menacing, and Nia wasn't sure how to respond.

For a moment, she felt like the proverbial deer stuck in the headlights.

She was all too aware of the bouncer behind her. Of the gun at his waist.

All too aware of how she and Gage were essentially trapped.

Aware of how they'd told no one where they'd be.

And she was all too aware of how she could end up on the floor with a fatal knife wound . . . just like Rob.

chapter
fourteen

GAGE PLACED his hand on Nia's back, sensing her panic.

He knew he needed to step in. Darius wasn't fully buying her cover story, and Gage didn't want things to turn ugly.

"The truth is that Rob Lesner was found dead in his apartment this morning," Gage told Darius. "We're friends of his, and we're trying to retrace his steps, see if anyone knows something."

He watched Darius's face carefully for any sign of deceit. But the surprise that flashed through the man's eyes looked genuine.

"Is that right?" Darius leaned back and steepled his hands in front of him as if taking time to process that statement. "I'm sorry to hear that, I guess."

"You guess?" Gage gave the man the opportunity to explain his statement.

He shrugged. "I was never a big fan of the guy."

"Because of Brittany?" Gage clarified.

Darius offered another half shrug. "The two of us were dating when Rob swooped in and stole her away from me. You don't intrude on another man's woman. He didn't play by the rules."

Did this guy have a set of unwritten "gentlemanly" rules? Because Darius didn't seem like a gentleman, that was for sure.

"I can imagine that upset you," Gage said.

He tilted his head analytically. "Are you saying something like that wouldn't upset you?"

"Not at all. I wouldn't want any other guy trying to steal my girl. The question is, would it make me mad enough to commit murder?" Gage's words were risky.

They could put the man into fight mode.

Or they could lead Darius to answer some questions.

"You think I murdered that man? *That's* really why you're both here?" Darius let out a long, deep chuckle. "I'll tell you this—Brittany was nothing but trouble. Drama follows her like ducklings following their mom. Sure, she was eye candy and something nice to have on my arm. But she was too much trouble. I was glad Rob took her off my hands."

"So you weren't mad?" Nia narrowed her gaze as she studied the man.

Gage understood her surprise. Brittany had made it sound like Darius was still in love with her. Their stories didn't match up.

"I didn't say that. But the man wasn't worth my time, and he certainly wasn't worth going away for life.

Now, do you have any other questions?" Darius raised his eyebrows as he glanced at them.

Gage knew they were done here. "That will be all."

As they turned to walk away, Gage felt the shudder ripple through Nia.

Whatever she'd gotten herself involved with, she was in way over her head.

Nia paused, trying to catch her breath after she stepped outside Avenue 12.

Darius Miller was dangerous. She'd felt the tension in the air as soon as she walked into his establishment.

Gage looked equally bothered.

He led her away from the bouncer before pausing and rubbing his jaw. His gaze hardened as he said, "Rob wasn't the type to steal another man's girlfriend."

That was an interesting statement. But that was the sense Nia had gotten about Rob. He seemed like a stand-up guy.

"You think Darius was lying?" she asked.

Gage rubbed his jaw as he stared down the street. "I don't know. But something's not adding up."

"What do we do now?"

He did a double take at the question.

Nia had said *we*.

How would Gage react? Would he try to send her away?

The truth was, neither of them were investigators. Both were in over their heads.

But both of them wanted answers and wouldn't have any peace in their lives until they knew the truth.

Though Nia hadn't told Gage everything yet, her involvement might seem unusual. But she hoped she could sell her cover story.

Gage placed his hand on Nia's back again—something that was quickly becoming familiar—and began to walk down the sidewalk. The scent of the ocean wafted toward them, along with the aromas of a nearby food truck. Grilled chicken and onions, she would guess. Reggae music played from somewhere in the distance.

Her thoughts drifted as she tried to sort out her feelings.

Maybe she should come clean with Gage. He seemed like a decent enough guy. And he seemed truly concerned for his friend.

Maybe if the two of them worked together . . . if she could really trust him . . .

As they joined a small crowd at a crosswalk, she licked her lips.

There wasn't an easy way to say this, so she might as well get it over with.

She quickly glanced at him as she tried to gather her courage. "Gage, I just feel like I should tell you—"

But before she could finish the statement, a bullet sliced the air.

People around her screamed and ran for cover.

The next second, another bullet flew.

Someone was shooting at them, she realized.

Her head spun at the thought.

She needed to move.

To do something.

Instead, she felt frozen and confused.

What if the next bullet hit its target . . . ?

What if it hit her?

chapter
fifteen

"WE NEED TO MOVE!" Gage grabbed Nia's arm and pulled her away.

Nia stifled another scream but didn't fight him.

Those bullets were meant for *them*.

He was certain of it.

Based on the trajectory, the gunman was somewhere on the street not far away.

Most likely, this guy would continue to pursue them. His moves were brazen.

They needed to get somewhere safe—and fast.

He kept a hand on Nia's arm as he pulled her down the sidewalk.

Did this have something to do with Rob's death?

Or had an enemy from Gage's past found him?

He had many. More than he could count, for that matter. So many people wanted him dead that it wasn't even funny, despite the jokes he and his colleagues made about it.

Or . . . this person could be someone Darius had sent after them. Maybe they were getting too close to answers. Maybe they'd spooked him.

But Gage didn't have time to figure that out now.

Right now, he needed to get Nia to safety.

And . . . he needed answers from Nia before someone killed her.

The thought seemed callous, and he didn't exactly mean it that way. Part of him wanted to believe she was innocent. But he couldn't allow himself to do that. He couldn't allow himself to be vulnerable.

Training 101 for his job: *always keep walls up. Self-preservation is everything.*

It was the only way he'd survived some of his missions.

Off-book missions the military had sent him on.

Missions where, if Gage was caught, the government would claim to have no knowledge of who he was or what he was doing.

They'd been risky, to say the least.

But he'd been trained for them as a super soldier of sorts.

As another bullet flew through the air, he pulled Nia faster. This guy was following them and making no secret of it.

"This way!" Gage tugged her into a nearby office building.

The receptionist behind the white marble desk looked at them with wide eyes as they ran by. "Excuse me . . . can I help you?"

But they moved too fast for anyone to stop them.

Gage knew he was only buying time.

The gunman would follow them inside this place in a matter of seconds.

"Where are we going?" Nia's voice sounded breathless as Gage led her down a hallway.

"We just need to get away." He turned around another corner down another hallway.

"There should be an exit somewhere close by."

They could leave this building and head across the street to another. They could keep doing that until they lost this guy.

But as they reached the end of the hallway, a window stared back.

A window that was sealed shut.

"Gage . . ." Nia stared at it.

His thoughts raced.

He only had mere seconds before that gunman would appear. He could hear the footsteps running in the distance, right around the corner.

Gage had a gun, but he didn't want to pull it out. Didn't want to show his hand . . . yet.

His cover would be blown if he did.

But he'd draw his Sig if it came down to it.

Nia's heart raced out of control.

How were she and Gage going to get out of this one?

They were trapped inside this building.

She glanced at Gage, hoping he might have some sort of plan. His sharp gaze showed he was trying to compute his next move.

It was almost like . . . he knew what he was doing.

She swallowed hard at the thought.

Exactly who was this guy? A computer repair tech? He hardly seemed like it.

The shooter appeared at the end of the hallway.

"This way!" Gage grabbed her arm again and pulled her to a nearby doorway.

He twisted the knob, and the door opened.

They slipped inside. Numerous people sitting at cubicles looked up and stared at them in confusion.

"Don't mind us," Gage muttered before darting through the office space.

Sweat spread across Nia's forehead with every step.

Would this guy follow them and finish them off?

How many of these people would become collateral damage?

Hopefully, none of them.

Right now, they were buying time.

More time meant more possibilities to figure something out.

Just ahead, Nia spotted a door leading outside.

She released her breath.

She hadn't realized this office had a separate entrance to the building. But it made sense.

And it could be a lifesaver.

"Hey!" someone in the office yelled. "What do you think you're doing?"

Gage ignored them and guided Nia to the door.

They burst outside and onto another city street.

She sucked in air, trying to catch her breath.

People around them stared.

They were probably a sight to see.

But Nia knew this wasn't over yet.

That guy . . . he'd find them at any minute.

She glanced up at Gage, still chugging in deep gulps of air. "What are we going to do now? We can't just stand here."

Gage's gaze stopped on something in the distance. "There!"

He pulled her toward a delivery truck that had just started to drive away.

A delivery truck? Certainly, he wasn't thinking . . .

People only did things like this in the movies.

Yet just as the truck was about to take off, he grabbed the cargo door and jerked it open. The next moment, he jumped onto the back of it, dragging Nia with him.

As the truck headed down the street, the gunman burst from the office and onto the sidewalk.

A man with broad shoulders and blond hair stared at them, a grimace on his face.

More than a grimace.

It was a promise to finish what he'd started.

chapter
sixteen

GAGE WAS careful to keep a hand on Nia as they headed down the city street in the back of the delivery truck. Plastic pallets filled with loaves of bread set on portable shelves surrounded them, along with the scent of yeast.

There was still a possibility this guy could catch them.

Gage hadn't recognized the guy—but the man certainly seemed to know who they were. He was targeting them.

But why? There were too many possibilities.

Nia looked over at him as she gripped the edge of the door. "What is this about?"

"I'm not sure." He pulled his gaze away from her and peered out the back window again.

"What aren't you telling me?" she rushed.

Based on the tone of her voice, she didn't trust him.

He looked back at her, the truck bouncing them both. "What aren't *you* telling *me*?"

The two of them stared off.

Finally, Gage licked his lips. "Whatever is going on, we need to stick together. That guy was shooting at both of us, and he's not done yet."

Nia went pale at his words, and she gripped the shelf beside her. "So what do we need to do next?"

That was an excellent question. It wasn't safe to go back to her apartment.

"We need to find somewhere safe to lie low for a while," he muttered. "I'm not sure where yet."

Peering out the back, Gage spotted the gunman again. The man ran along the sidewalk after them, appearing ready to shoot at any minute.

Then the truck turned.

They were out of the direct line of fire. For now.

Gage grabbed his phone.

If anyone could help, it was Alan Larchmont, his boss at the Shadow Agency. The man had endless resources, and strategy seemed to come second nature to him.

The two chatted several minutes. When he ended the call, Nia stared at him. A sheen of distrust filled her gaze, and her shoulders looked tighter than they had before.

"Who were you talking to?" Her words sounded clipped as she asked the question.

"My boss." He slid the phone back into his pocket and peered behind them again.

No sign of the guy.

"At the computer repair company?" She said the words slowly, skeptically.

"He's going to help find us a place to hide out. He's resourceful."

Nia eyed him another moment before asking, "Okay . . . so what did this resourceful boss recommend we do?"

If Gage really was stuck with Nia for a while, he needed to make the best of things. He needed to use the time to his advantage. Needed to find out answers.

That meant instead of getting rid of her, he needed to get to know her. Needed to find out what she knew. Needed to get her to trust him.

Finally, Gage locked gazes with her and said, "We're going to track down a killer."

The truck stopped at a red light, and Nia's heart pounded harder.

Would the gunman catch up?

Before she could think about it too much, Gage grabbed Nia's hand. "We gotta go!"

He pulled her off and their feet hit the pavement with a thud.

She glanced around.

No signs of danger.

Not yet.

They'd probably gone four city blocks in the truck, so maybe they'd lost him—at least, for a while.

Gage kept a grip on her hand—purely for practical

reasons no doubt—and led her quickly across the street. He seemed to know exactly what he was doing.

They stepped into the Royal Oasis, one of the swanky hotels in the area. From what Nia heard, the rooms at this place cost more than a thousand per night.

Despite that, Gage strode to the front desk, acting as if he stayed in places like this often. "I should have a reservation for Henry Grimshaw."

A reservation? Whose name had he just given?

Nia glanced behind her, her back muscles tight. She halfway expected the gunman to burst into the hotel and follow them.

But so far so good.

The clerk checked his computer before smiling at Gage. "Of course, Mr. Grimshaw." He slid a key card across the counter. "Here you go. Take the elevator to the eighth floor. Your room should be ready."

Nia had a million questions. But she didn't voice any out loud until she and Gage were on the elevator alone.

"How did you get this reservation so quickly?" she rushed. "Or is this where you were planning on staying while you were in town? Whose name are you using?"

"My boss set this up for me," Gage said. "Like I said, he's resourceful. We need to go someplace safe where no one can track either of us. That means we can't use our real names."

That nauseous feeling roiled in her gut again. What exactly was going on here? Nia had so many questions. Yet she didn't even know where to start or what to ask. Not really.

She'd never been in a situation even remotely like this in all her thirty-two years.

They reached the eighth floor surprisingly fast.

Before stepping out of the elevator, Gage checked the hallway. Then they started toward the room. He slipped the card into the lock, listened as it buzzed, and a moment later, they were inside.

Nia took a moment to appreciate the beautiful suite. One that looked fit for royalty with its exquisite living room area that featured a creamy couch and chairs, luscious ivory curtains, and numerous glass-topped tables. Three doors lined the walls in the distance, probably bedrooms and a bathroom.

But she didn't have a chance to appreciate the space very long.

Gage grabbed a chair and leaned it against the door. He then secured all the locks.

Nia knew what that meant.

That meant there was still a chance this gunman could find them.

Her throat went dry at the thought.

As soon as he'd secured the door, Gage scurried around the rest of the suite and checked out every nook and cranny.

Nia stood against the wall and watched, unsure what else to do.

She wanted to trust Gage.

But she didn't know if that was wise. She still had questions.

Things didn't make sense.

Finally, he motioned to her. "Let's sit down. We have a lot to talk about."

Nia nodded and forced herself to walk farther into the space. Gage grabbed some water and snacks from the kitchenette on the way past.

Good. She was thirsty and hadn't even realized it until now.

The two of them headed toward the living room. Gage placed the drinks and snacks on the coffee table and motioned to her to take one. Nia grabbed a water, twisted the top off, and took a long sip.

Before lowering himself to the couch, Gage stripped off his outer shirt and tossed it on a chair. He glanced at his forearm where a trickle of blood ran down it.

Somewhere along the way, he'd cut himself.

"You okay?" Nia asked.

He nodded. "It's not deep. I just need to clean it in a moment."

Nia sat on the loveseat perpendicular to him, still shivering from the adrenaline rush.

He raked a hand through his wavy hair, leaving it on end.

Gage was shaken by all this, too, wasn't he?

As he shifted again, his shirt sleeve rose.

A tattoo high on his bicep came into sight.

The same tattoo she'd seen on the man in Rob's apartment after he died.

The blood drained from her face.

Gage *did* have secrets. Big secrets.

He'd already known Rob was dead when he showed up at her place.

He'd already been inside the apartment. Seen the body.

And he'd been leading her on, making her believe he was clueless.

The truth was . . . *he* was the dangerous one here.

Had he killed Rob and set it up to look like she'd done it? Then maybe he'd left for some reason and come back only to find her gone.

Had he only kept her alive today because he needed something from her?

But the texts. She'd gotten one while Gage was with her . . .

Maybe Gage was working with someone. His supposed boss? Was this all a setup?

Nia's heart thumped in her ears.

At the first opportunity, she needed to lose him.

Her life might depend on it.

chapter
seventeen

GAGE COULD SEE Nia was still visibly shaken. Instead of calming down in the safety of the hotel room, her nerves seemed to kick in even more.

He nodded at her water, encouraging her to drink more. The last thing he needed was for her to pass out.

Not with that guy after them.

He'd committed the man's image to his memory.

Gage was nearly certain the gunman was part of Dagger, a rival private security agency—one with less than honorable tactics. Many Dagger members were former special forces. Or they were guys who *had been* special forces before being kicked off their teams for inappropriate behaviors.

He'd encountered Dagger before, and he knew those agents would do whatever was asked of them—for the right price.

It was a miracle he and Nia hadn't been shot.

Were those guys responsible for Rob's death?

Or was this unrelated?

He needed more information before he could draw any conclusions.

"What are we going to do?" Nia's voice sounded scratchy.

"I wish I had my computer with me, but I don't. I'll need to use my phone." He began typing something onto the screen.

"What are you looking up?" She squinted as if desperate to see, to know his thoughts.

"I want to look into Darius and Brittany. I sent an email asking some colleagues of mine to investigate them also. Several of them are excellent at researching things on the web and getting into sites that others don't even know exist. I want to find out all we can about them."

"Do you think either Brittany or Darius is responsible for Rob's death?" Nia cocked her head to the side as she waited for his answer.

Gage shrugged and kept typing on his phone. "Right now, I'm just gathering information. I honestly don't know. But Darius and Brittany are our best leads. I mean, I don't have anyone else in mind. Do you?"

She frowned. "I guess not."

"Then we start by ruling them out, and then move on if it's not one of them."

Nia tucked her legs beneath her and took a couple more sips of water. "So the people who shot at us were somehow connected with Darius or Brittany?"

Gage swallowed hard, trying to stick with the truth. He didn't want to tell Nia there was a possibility trouble had followed him here. That those gunmen could be after *him*.

After all, it didn't make sense that gunman would go after Nia. She was most likely the killer.

It didn't make sense right now, at least.

"There's a good possibility they were hired." He glanced at his phone screen, still waiting for results. "That maybe when we talked to Darius, he got spooked."

Nia rubbed her throat and stared out the window as if lost in thought. "I feel like I'm tangled in a web I won't ever get out of."

"If you get caught in a web, all you have to do is cut the line. You might drag part of the fibers with you, and they might slow you down, but at least you won't be trapped anymore."

She stared at him another moment before nodding. "Interesting perspective."

Gage's phone rang. It was his former colleague Jonah Gray. Gage had called to ask for his assistance earlier. Even though Jonah wasn't officially with the Shadow Agency anymore, Gage knew he could depend on Jonah. The two had been friends for years.

"Any updates on who killed Rob?" Jonah asked.

His friend had heard him talk about Rob before and knew how close the two were. Jonah had lost a childhood friend last year, so he understood the pain of it.

He glanced at Nia again. He didn't say the words aloud, but she was still the one who made the most sense as the killer.

Even if she did look vulnerable and scared as she sat across from him.

Gage cleared his throat. "I have someone in my sights. Someone I want to explore."

"Then you should keep all your options open."

He continued to stare at her. "That's what I plan on doing. But I'm going to have to talk to you more later. You got the picture I sent, right?"

He'd sent his friend a picture of the knife used to kill Rob. It seemed like it could be significant. Jonah had a connection, an old friend who collected knives. Gage hoped Jonah might talk to his friend and find out anything noteworthy about the weapon.

He glanced at Nia again.

If Nia was behind this, then Gage would find out . . . if it was the last thing he did.

What was that conversation about? Nia wondered.

There was *definitely* more to Gage Pearson than he let on.

She'd been a fool to trust him even a little.

In fact, what if this had actually been a setup? She couldn't shake the thought from her head. What if that gunman had purposefully missed them? Just so she would trust Gage? So she would come here with him?

After all, she already knew he'd been in Rob's apartment.

It was twisted . . . like something from the plot of some action-adventure movie.

But this was real life.

Whatever happened with Rob, Nia still couldn't remember any of it. For all she knew, Gage had been a part of last night's deadly shenanigans. Maybe he'd killed Rob, framed her, and then come back to plant more evidence.

Or maybe he'd killed Rob and now he wanted something from her.

Information on the app Rob was developing? What if someone else wanted to profit from it?

Nia didn't know. But her thoughts rushed so quickly she felt like she might pass out.

At the first chance, she'd escape.

And what then? That gunman could still be out there, waiting to finish her off.

There was so much she didn't know.

The only solution was to find out answers about Rob.

"What are you thinking?" Gage shifted before taking another sip of his drink.

Nia didn't dare tell him the whole truth. "I want to know what happened in the time between when Rob met with me at the office and when he called around four to set up dinner. Something appears to have spooked him."

"I agree. We need to figure out what that was."

She nibbled on her lip as she thought. She needed to make it sound as if she was working with Gage still, even though she planned on escaping as soon as possible. "I wish we had access to his phone or his files. That might tell us something."

"The police have those. They're not going to share any of that information with us. What about this Sigmund guy you mentioned earlier? The other tech broker trying to woo Rob?"

Nia sighed and shrugged. "I don't know what there is to say. The guy is a good businessman and my biggest competition. But not necessarily a killer. He's smart enough to know that contract was iron-clad."

"Then who else could it be?"

"The only other people I can think of to talk to are Hector, Rob's lawyer, or Cormac."

Nia watched Gage's face to see if he recognized Cormac's name. If the two of them were truly friends, he would.

"His friend and assistant?" Gage said. "Yes, I'm surprised he hasn't been around."

"Rob mentioned yesterday something about Cormac having a trip planned, so he could be out of town. Otherwise, I'd think we would have seen him today."

"Agreed. I think we should pursue both of those angles." He paused, his gaze drifting in the distance with thought. "I'm still curious about Brittany and Darius as well. I can't believe Rob didn't tell me he was dating someone."

"And Darius definitely seems suspicious, like someone you don't want to get on the wrong side of."

Gage stood. "It sounds like we have some good places

to start. I just need to clean up this cut. Give me ten, and we can leave."

Nia's heart skipped a beat. This was her chance to escape.

She kept her voice even as she said, "Sounds like a plan."

As soon as Gage disappeared into the bathroom, Nia quietly stood. Not making a sound, she walked to the door, moved the chair, and turned the locks.

Hesitating only a moment, she twisted the knob.

Opened the door.

Glanced up and down the hallway.

Empty.

Nia looked back at the closed bathroom door one more time. She could still hear the water running inside.

She'd really wanted to trust Gage. Wanted to believe he was one of the good guys.

But trusting him had been a mistake.

Quietly closing the door behind her, Nia jostled into action.

She darted down the hallway and punched the button to the elevator. As she waited, her heart fluttered out of control.

She glanced back down at the doorway, halfway expecting Gage to emerge.

He didn't.

Finally, the elevator dinged.

It was empty.

Temporary relief filled her, but she couldn't afford to let down her guard.

She rushed inside and hit the button for the lobby. As the elevator doors closed, she prayed it didn't stop on any other floors, that no one else stepped inside.

Images of that gunman filled her thoughts.

What if he found her? Cornered her here in the elevator?

What would she do if that happened?

She didn't know.

But she knew she wasn't safe with Gage either.

She was better off taking her chances on her own.

chapter
eighteen

AS SOON AS Gage opened the bathroom door, he froze.

The chair was no longer wedged underneath the handle of the door leading into the room. Instead, it had been tossed aside.

He reached for his gun and cautiously stepped out. He scanned the room.

No one was there—not even Nia.

Nor were there any signs of foul play.

If there had been an incident, he would have heard something. Even though the water from the sink could have concealed some sounds, his ears were attuned for signs of danger.

Nia had left on her own, hadn't she?

Gage muttered beneath his breath.

He shouldn't have left her alone. But he thought he'd earned her trust.

What had spooked her? What had caused her to go

out on her own with a gunman out there trying to track them down?

His jaw tightened, and tension thrummed through his muscles.

Gage had to find her before too much time passed.

Before someone else found her first.

Drawing in a deep breath, he stepped toward the door.

He'd probably only been in the bathroom for seven or eight minutes. But that was long enough for Nia to get too far away for his comfort.

He took the elevator to the lobby, stepped out, and glanced around.

No Nia.

No gunman either. At least *that* was good news.

A few minutes later, he paused on the sidewalk and scanned the city streets.

Still no Nia.

Where would she have gone?

That was what he needed to figure out.

Nia hadn't known where to go. So she'd gone into work.

She'd gotten some curious looks from her co-workers when she rushed inside, but she largely ignored them and escaped into her office instead. Since she was the boss, no one had questioned her. She'd given instructions to Melissa, her assistant, that she didn't want to see anyone or take any calls.

But now she was in her office, and she felt restless.

She kept glancing at the door, halfway expecting Gage to show up.

But he didn't.

When she wasn't glancing at the door, she was staring out her window.

But she didn't see anyone suspicious or watching her from outside either.

Had she somehow managed to lose that guy?

It almost seemed too good to be true.

One thing was certain—she couldn't just sit here.

She needed to find answers.

Her thoughts went back to the meeting Rob had here at the office. She'd been a part of it, as well as her VP, Graham Boston, and her Director of Development, Keith Washington. They'd met in the conference room, and Rob had truly seemed excited about the deal they'd brokered.

He'd left here at two-thirty. At four, he'd called about dinner.

What had happened in that time to change his mood from excited to anxious?

Nia tapped her finger on her desk as she thought it through.

Right as Rob had been leaving her office, he'd gotten a text, she remembered. He'd frowned as he looked at the screen. Nia hadn't thought much about his reaction at the time. But what if that text was the start of his trouble?

If only she had access to his phone . . .

She continued to tap her finger.

She *did* have some capabilities for hacking into certain online accounts. Her company had brokered many deals in the tech world. As part of that, they kept prototypes and paperwork in the office as a backup.

And some of her clients had developed extraordinary technology and programs for both the private sector and the government.

She could dive into some of that tech to find out information she needed. But if she were caught . . .

The key would be not being caught, she supposed.

She turned to her computer as she contemplated what she should do.

chapter
nineteen

NIA LEANED back in her chair as she waited for Chatterbox to work.

Chatterbox had almost been sold to police departments across the country—before a judge had ruled it illegal and the project had been shelved. However, Nia still had the prototype.

The program was brilliant, really. When someone entered a phone number, Chatterbox pulled call records. The creator's hope was that it could help law enforcement skip getting a warrant and going through phone companies to get these records in time-sensitive investigations.

Just don't get caught.

That was what she kept telling herself.

As she waited, she tried to call Hector Backus, Rob's attorney.

The call went to voicemail. She'd try again later.

After several more minutes, a log of Rob's phone calls populated her screen.

Nia's breath caught.

Would this information pinpoint who the killer was?

If that was the case, what would she do with whatever she discovered?

Thirty minutes after Nia left, Gage figured out—through the process of elimination—where she'd gone.

She was too smart to go back to her apartment, and the cops were probably still at Rob's place.

Going back to Avenue 12 probably wouldn't provide any answers, and she didn't seem comfortable in that place to begin with.

She could have left the hotel and gone to talk to Rob's lawyer—not that the man would share anything with her. But Gage didn't think she'd done that.

The place that made the most sense was her office. Maybe Nia would look at her contract with Rob again. Talk to her employees to see if any of them had seen Rob after he left the office. Maybe she'd use some of the technology at her disposal.

Gage had bought a hat and some sunglasses from a street vendor and purchased a newspaper from a news rack on the corner. Then he found a spot across the street from Nia's office building where he could linger and pretend to read as he watched her window.

He'd done some research and knew which window

was hers. He could vaguely make out her figure at the desk behind the tinted glass.

With one shot, a skilled gunman could take her out.

His muscles tightened at the thought.

What had Nia been thinking? Why had she left when she did?

She was putting herself at risk.

Or she was acting as a cunning killer?

Gage wasn't sure which one yet. A frown tugged at his lips.

When he'd shown up at her apartment earlier, he'd seen some art on her wall by the entry. It was a picture of Jesus calming the storm. Below it had been the Scripture reference. Mark 4:39, *He got up, rebuked the wind, and said to the waves, "Quiet! Be still!" Then the wind died down and it was completely calm.*

Nia presented herself as a Christian—something Gage could appreciate. But he could only appreciate it if the walk and the talk matched.

Then again, he had no reason to talk.

The job he worked required subterfuge. Lies. Sometimes violence.

Who was he to judge someone else?

Maybe he needed to get his act together first.

He'd become a believer a few years ago, but he was never in the same place very long, so getting involved with a church community was difficult. At times, he struggled with what to do. To find balance in his life.

His phone buzzed, and he glanced at the screen.

Perfect. His colleague, Austin Greenwich, had just arrived in Miami and picked up a rental car.

Gage texted Austin his current location.

When he got there, they'd switch spots. Gage would let Austin keep an eye on Nia while Gage checked out a few other leads.

chapter
twenty

NIA QUICKLY SCANNED Rob's phone calls on the day he died.

Rob had made two to her and one to Gage.

At least *that* part of Gage's story was true. But it didn't prove the two of them truly had been friends. However, she had seen Gage call Rob while she'd been in the apartment after she'd found Rob dead.

The man confused her, made her feel uncertain.

She *hated* feeling uncertain.

Then there were the phone calls to Rob from an unknown number—at least eight of them. Nia jotted the digits down so she could search them. If Gage wasn't guilty, then could that unknown number belong to the killer?

The questions swirled in her head.

Then there were the calls from Brittany Stevens.

Nia scanned back several days and saw a lot of time had gone by between when the two talked. Not typical dating behavior. Usually if two people were together, she'd expect at least a couple of phone calls every day.

Something about their whole relationship didn't ring true with her.

She printed the call logs, folded them, and shoved them into her pocket.

Then she looked at Rob's text messages.

Most of them were inconsequential. A lot of them were just jokes back and forth with friends.

But Nia found the one he'd received right before he left the office after their meeting yesterday.

We need to talk.

She compared the numbers. The message was from the same caller with the unknown number.

Her back muscles pinched.

Rob had gotten that text, and it had upset him.

Then someone called from the same number only twenty minutes later.

That phone number was *definitely* a link she was looking for. But if this person was as smart as she thought, this number wouldn't lead back to anyone specific.

Then another thought struck her.

What if Gage had two phones? What if he called Rob on one for friendly conversations and used the other to make threats?

Even as she asked herself that question, it didn't

make sense. Rob would recognize Gage's voice no matter which phone he used.

Nia was reading too much into this, wasn't she? Maybe she was making it more complicated than it should be.

She continued to study the phone calls and texts for answers.

But it was like a puzzle. She just needed to figure out what pieces went where.

Gage left Austin standing guard on the sidewalk.

His colleague promised to let Gage know as soon as Nia left the building.

Meanwhile, Gage had several leads he wanted to look into.

Even though he believed Nia had something to do with this, there were a lot of other loose ends and unanswered questions.

Just as he and Nia had discussed—he needed to figure out what had happened in the time between when Nia had met with Rob at the office and when the two of them had dinner together.

Rob had left the office around two-thirty, called Gage around four-thirty, and met Nia at eight.

Something had gone wrong. If Rob had called Gage, there was a high probability Rob felt as if he were in danger.

Because dealing with danger was what Gage did.

Had something happened at the restaurant?

If only Gage had asked more questions when Rob called him . . . if only he knew then what he knew now.

The one other piece of this puzzle that didn't make any sense was Brittany.

Was Rob's murder really because of a bad breakup and a jealous ex-boyfriend? Gage found that hard to believe.

He wanted to talk to Brittany one-on-one.

He already had her address, and he'd taken Austin's rental car—which just happened to be a black Porsche 911—to head there now. Thankfully, her place wasn't far away so he could be back soon if Austin needed him for anything.

As he drove, Jonah called him, and he answered through Bluetooth.

"I had my friend look into that knife," Jonah started. "Unfortunately, there's nothing special about it. In fact, you can buy them on Amazon. This one in particular is known as a Viking. People who like to cook and have money use them. Sorry I can't be of more help."

Gage frowned. He'd been hoping for more. "Thanks. I appreciate you looking into it."

They chatted a few more minutes before ending the call.

The knife had been a dead end.

Hopefully, his new lead wouldn't be.

Minutes later, he parked in front of a smaller house on the outskirts of the city.

He'd expected something fancier for a woman like Brittany. But her accommodations didn't matter to him.

As he studied the house, he saw the curtain inside flutter.

Someone had seen him pull up.

Now he needed to make sure that someone talked to him.

chapter
twenty-one

GAGE KNOCKED AT THE DOOR.

No one answered.

He knocked again.

Still no answer.

He glanced at the old, beat-up sage-green Volvo in the driveway.

The vehicle looked like something Brittany might drive—but only in desperate circumstances. She seemed like more of a diva.

Still no answer at the door.

Gage let out a sigh. Why couldn't anything be easy?

Finally, he leaned closer and said, "Brittany, I know you're in there. Why don't you make this easier for all of us and come out? I just want to talk. I thought you wanted my help."

Silence passed.

Just when he was certain he'd have to bust down the door if he wanted to get inside, it opened.

But Brittany wasn't standing there.

The woman was an older version of Brittany, one with wrinkles, brittle blonde hair, and ill-fitting clothes. The sound of *Wheel of Fortune* blared in the background, and the smell of collard greens filled the air.

The leafy vegetable had been one of his grandmother's favorites, and Gage would recognize it anywhere.

The woman stared at him as she braced herself between the door and the doorway. "What do you want with my Brittany?"

Her voice sounded deep and throaty, like someone who'd smoked cigarettes for too many years.

"I'm Gage," he started. "Brittany asked me to help her figure out what happened to her boyfriend, Rob. You may have heard he died."

She nodded somberly. "I did. I was sorry to hear that."

"Me too. I had some follow-up questions for Brittany, more information I need to know."

The woman shook her head. "I'm Brittany's mom. She lives here with me. But she's not home right now. She's out with her friends—just like always."

Even right after her boyfriend was found dead? Gage swallowed the question. Partying after a loved one's death seemed disrespectful. But Gage still had doubts that Rob and Brittany had ever truly dated.

"If you don't mind me asking, what do Brittany and her friends do when they go out?" Gage asked instead.

Mrs. Stevens shrugged. "They party. I thought Brittany would outgrow it, but she never did. That's just who she is. That's what she always tells me, at least."

Gage's opinion of Brittany continued to shrink. "Do you know when she'll be back?"

"There's no telling. It could be any hour of the night. Or tomorrow even."

"Doesn't she have to go to work in the morning?" Gage wasn't sure what Brittany did for a living, but she wasn't college-aged anymore.

This woman was clearly aggravated with Brittany if she was telling Gage all this. But he wasn't going to complain.

"She doesn't work. Not really. I mean, on occasion she'll get a modeling job or something. But otherwise, she lives here rent-free and borrows my car. I buy the food and pay the bills. Really, all she needs money for is clothes and having a good time." The woman frowned. "I know what you're thinking. And don't judge me."

"I'm not judging you." Gage softened his voice. "I'm just trying to put some pieces together. Did you know Rob?"

Her expression softened ever so slightly. "Never met him. Only heard Brittany talk about him."

"I'm trying to figure out how long they dated."

The woman let out a raspy laugh. "Maybe two weeks."

"That's all?" Gage had the impression the two of them had been an item for a while. Brittany's reaction at Rob's apartment after he died had been over-the-top for such a short relationship.

But that didn't surprise him. Mostly because Brittany, in general, seemed over-the-top.

"Rob told her he just didn't see the two of them going anywhere," Mrs. Stevens continued.

Gage straightened at the statement. "When did he say that?"

She shrugged. "A couple of days ago. Brittany came home crying and dug into some rocky road ice cream to comfort herself."

So Brittany hadn't told Gage the complete truth. Not that Gage was surprised. But why would she lie about her relationship with Rob? What did she stand to gain by not telling the truth?

"I heard that Darius was jealous." Gage might as well ask more questions while the woman was talking.

Mrs. Stevens let out a coughing laugh. "I don't know about that. Part of me thinks he was ready to get rid of her. In my opinion? Brittany is the one who wants him back and not vice versa."

Gage stored that information away.

There was clearly more to the story.

Gage needed to figure out how Rob fit into it all.

Just as Nia thought, the caller with the unknown number had used a burner.

She wouldn't get any information about who had bought it. At least not easily.

That left her back at square one.

She *could* still try to track down Hector, Rob's attorney. She just might do that.

But as of right now, she didn't have any more answers.

She'd noticed that one of Rob's frequent phone calls and texts had been from Cormac. She still needed to locate him. She'd tried calling, but there had been no answer.

She had his address also. If she could get out of her office and find the courage to do so, she could try to track him down and question him. She could see if he was really out of town or not.

The problem was getting out of here.

She glanced out the window. Darkness had fallen outside. The days in February were short, and she missed the sunshine. At least in Miami it wasn't cold.

A knock sounded at her door, and she called, "Come in!"

Melissa peeked her head inside, an apologetic look in her eyes. "Graham insists on talking to you. He won't take no for an answer."

Nia frowned but nodded. "Send him in."

A moment later, Graham stepped inside. The man was in his late forties with thinning light-brown hair and a body and physique that showed he worked way too much overtime in the office. Yet the guy was skilled and did the tasks Nia didn't want to do.

"I'm headed home for the night," he announced. "Anything you need?"

"No, nothing," she told him. "I'll be leaving in a few minutes."

He studied her a moment. "Are you okay? You seem a little jumpy. And your clothes . . ." He gave her a look of disdain.

She forced a smile. "I'm fine. Thank you."

His gaze lingered on her a moment longer before he closed the door.

Nia released her breath now that he was gone. Then she turned her thoughts back to how she would get out of here.

Though Nia was tempted to camp out here tonight, she knew she couldn't stay at work forever.

But it didn't seem safe to go back to her apartment. So where could she go?

She could rent a hotel room, but if someone was smart enough or resourceful enough, they could track her credit card, and she didn't have enough cash on hand to pay that way.

Besides, time was of the essence right now. At any time, she expected to receive another text. A demand.

She needed to figure out those answers before the gunman found her again.

Or Gage found her.

All she needed to do was make it to her car, which she'd left in the garage located next to the office building.

If she could make it there, she would be out of sight and safe.

In theory.

But what if the gunman was in the garage waiting for her?

Still, courage wasn't the absence of fear. Courage was moving forward even when feeling afraid.

Nia couldn't remember who said the quote, but she knew deep in her bones that the words were true.

Because right now, she was terrified. But she grabbed what she needed from the office and placed one foot in front of the other as she stepped into the unknown.

chapter
twenty-two

GAGE ARRIVED BACK in downtown Miami, parked, and found Austin still standing on the sidewalk overlooking Nia's workplace.

"No movements since you left," his friend informed him.

"Good to know," Gage murmured. "Thanks for coming and doing this for me."

"Of course. What else can I do?" Austin shifted, ready to help out however he could. He'd proven himself to be a good friend.

"I need you to trace the whereabouts of this woman." Gage pulled out his phone and found a picture of Brittany. "I'll send you her information, including her address. But watch her socials. She seems like the type to post too much."

"I've met that type before."

"Haven't we all? Anyway, keep an eye on her. See where she goes. Who she talks to."

The woman had a reason for lying, and Gage wanted to figure out what that was.

"I can do that." Austin nodded slowly.

"I also want to talk to Rob's assistant, a guy named Cormac Westerly. I need you to track down his address and see if he's in town or not."

"Will do." Austin glanced up at Gage and narrowed his gaze. "What will you be doing?"

He nodded at Nia's office. "I'm going to keep an eye on her. She's my number one suspect."

Austin followed his gaze to the third floor and let out an approving whistle. "If you need to keep an eye on someone, she's the one you want to watch."

Gage narrowed his eyes. "It's not like that."

"This is purely business?" Austin raised his eyebrows.

"Purely business," Gage echoed.

Austin didn't look as if he believed him, but he nodded anyway. "Got it."

A moment later, his colleague climbed into the Porsche and pulled away.

Gage glanced up at Nia's office again. Though he couldn't see her right now, he remembered watching her at her desk earlier.

She *was* beautiful.

But potentially deadly also. He needed to keep his distance from the woman while also keeping her in his sights. He had no other choice.

Gage stood against the building, trying to appear as if he were simply playing on his phone. But his gaze continually flickered to Nia's office.

She still wasn't back.

Then he scanned the street.

Ten minutes after he sent Austin away, someone across the street caught his eye.

Gage's heart thumped harder.

It was him. The gunman who'd been chasing them earlier. Still wearing black slacks and a white T-shirt. A Miami Dolphins ballcap covered his head, concealing much of his face.

Gage could see the bulge at the back of his shirt— a gun.

This guy had figured out where Nia had gone.

Now it was only a matter of time before he made his next move.

Gage glanced at the time.

Six p.m. It was dark now, and darkness always seemed to side with the enemy. It made it easier to hide, to conceal things, to keep secrets.

A lot had happened since Gage had gotten to Miami. A lot had happened since he'd had coffee with Nia this morning, for that matter.

Did she plan on staying at work all night?

As if on cue, the light in Nia's office went dark.

She was about to leave.

Gage had seen her car in the parking garage. If he had to guess, that was where she'd go.

The gunman seemed to know that too and headed that direction.

Quickly, Gage fell into step behind him. He didn't want to make his presence known.

But he needed to stop this guy before he hurt Nia.

The gunman exchanged a look with someone across the street.

Gage saw the man and sucked in a breath. These two were working together.

Were they targeting Nia?

It was too early to say.

How many of these guys were there?

More tension stretched between Gage's shoulders.

He had to figure out what they were planning before someone else was hurt.

~

Nia made it to the skybridge between her office building and the parking garage without noticing anyone suspicious.

However, as soon as she stepped into the garage, something in the air changed.

Danger, invisible to her, followed her every step. She didn't see anyone specific. But she could sense peril closing in.

Leaving by herself had been a bad idea. She should have called security to escort her. But she'd feared they'd ask questions. Report her suspicious behavior to police.

What had she been thinking?

Of course, right now, everything seemed like a bad idea. Being on her own. Being with Gage. Being at her apartment. Being anywhere.

She'd run out of options.

She felt so exposed here.

Maybe she should turn around and go back to her office.

That was what she'd do.

She would go back, she decided. She'd barricade herself inside until she figured something else out.

She took a step back when a footstep echoed in the distance.

Her throat tightened until she felt as if she couldn't breathe.

She wasn't alone.

She took another step back, nearly falling. She caught herself.

A step sounded behind her also. So quiet it was almost ghostlike. But it was definitely there.

She couldn't go back into the office. She needed another plan.

She glanced around the parking garage, still seeing no signs of movement.

Maybe if she could make it to her car fast enough . . .

It was her only option.

She had to move. Otherwise, the guy behind her would reveal himself.

Wasting no more time, she darted to the right.

She sprinted past various cars in the dim space, suddenly wishing she hadn't parked on the far side of the garage.

As she passed a concrete pillar, someone stepped out.

A hand pressed over her mouth. An arm reached around her midsection, locking her limbs in place.

This was it, wasn't it?

She would die without any answers.

And Nia would have no one to blame but herself.

chapter
twenty-three

GAGE LEANED CLOSER TO NIA. "It's me. Don't make a sound. Understand?"

Some of the tension seemed to leave Nia, but she remained stiff.

"Understand?" Gage repeated.

She nodded.

"There are two guys in the garage coming for you," he whispered. "We don't have time to run. We need to hide."

Nia nodded again, though the action was rigid.

Releasing her slowly, Gage then took her hand. "Stay low."

He began pulling her toward a line of vehicles parked against the exterior wall of the building. He'd already scoped out the best escape plan.

He led her past several before stopping by a large black SUV, one that wasn't too new or too old.

One that blended in.

But he didn't open the door.

Instead, he motioned beneath it. "We're going under."

Nia's eyes widened.

A shout in the distance propelled her into action.

She scrambled beneath it. Gage followed behind.

Just as Gage pulled his leg out of sight, footsteps sounded on the pavement nearby.

Gage kept his head pressed to the gritty pavement. He ignored the scent of tar and motor oil. Ignored the tight space. Ignored the fact Nia stared at him, silently asking him questions.

The footsteps padded closer.

Stopped.

Gage spotted black, combat-style boots and tensed.

This guy was *definitely* one of the gunmen.

No doubt he was looking for them.

The man would probably assume Gage and Nia had gotten inside a car, and that would be the first place he looked.

Hopefully.

Nia drew in a shaky breath beside him, remaining perfectly still.

Her fear was real.

Nia didn't strike him as a cold-blooded killer. The thought hit him again.

Her fear right now reinforced it.

But that didn't mean she hadn't taken Rob's life. Maybe someone had manipulated her into doing it.

Maybe it had been out of self-defense. Maybe an accident.

Gage didn't know.

But he'd find out.

The man began walking again.

Paced closer.

Paused in front of the SUV.

Gage's heart pounded harder.

Then he reached for the gun at his waist, ready to use it if he had to.

Nia could hardly breathe.

That guy was going to find them and shoot them.

It was only a matter of time before he leaned down and spotted them beneath the SUV.

Her pulse thrummed harder and harder until she felt certain everyone around her could hear it.

Gage seemed like a smart man. But how would he get them out of this situation?

He had seemed so trustworthy.

But she'd seen his tattoo.

She knew he was lying to her.

How could she possibly trust him?

She couldn't.

Besides, what kind of computer repair tech carried a gun? And looked like he knew how to use it? Not just like he *knew* how to use it but like he was *comfortable* using it?

Nia's emotions and logic played tug of war inside her.

"I don't know where she went," the gunman muttered—maybe he was on his phone. "But I'll find her and take care of her. She couldn't have gotten but so far . . ."

A chill raced up her spine. That man was talking about her. About taking care of *her*.

This wasn't about Gage or anyone else.

A lump formed in her throat.

Seconds ticked by in slow motion.

Finally, the man paced away.

Nia wanted to feel relieved, but she couldn't. It was too soon.

Her earlier theory that Gage was trying to earn her trust because he had an ulterior motive filled her mind.

If that was the case, why would he crawl under this vehicle with her?

Nothing made sense right now. Nothing at all.

She wanted to press her eyes closed. To disappear. To pretend this wasn't happening.

But she couldn't do that.

The guy paced back toward them—pausing again near the SUV. As she glanced to the side, she saw his dirty black boots. The tightly tied laces. The mud on the edges of the soles.

What was he doing? Was he peering inside?

Maybe.

Her throat tightened.

All he had to do was to lean down and . . .

Somewhere in the distance, a car door opened.

Sirens wailed.

Outside the garage.

Would that cause this guy to act faster? Or would it cause him to run?

That was the question.

chapter
twenty-four

GAGE HEARD THE SIRENS. Had someone called the police?

He didn't know who would do that or why. Austin should be gone, and he had no idea about any of this.

Most likely, the sirens were unrelated.

Still, he froze and waited.

Hopefully, the sound had these guys spooked. They knew law enforcement was close. Would they chance sticking around?

Gage didn't think so.

He turned his head to check on Nia.

Her eyes were wide with fear, but she was okay.

However, the terror in her gaze was enough to make him want to murmur words of comfort.

But he didn't. He couldn't chance it.

One slight sound could give them away.

The minutes ticked by in slow motion.

Finally, the sound of footsteps fleeing caught his ear.

Gage's lungs loosened—just slightly.

This should buy him and Nia some time.

But he still needed to plan his next moves carefully.

Even if Nia had a car in the garage, there was a good chance a tracking device had been placed on it at this point. It wouldn't be safe to take the vehicle anywhere.

Gage had another idea. It wasn't his favorite. But in situations like this, he had little choice.

Right now, he wanted to stay alive.

He waited several moments. Then he carefully slid out from beneath the SUV and scanned the parking garage.

He didn't see the gunmen. They must have fled.

He knelt down. "It's safe. For now. You can come out."

She scooted out from beneath the SUV. Dirt and oil smudged her cheeks and clothing. She looked pale—too pale. Her breathing too shallow.

As long as she remained upright, none of that mattered.

Only surviving.

"Come with me." He grabbed her hand to ensure she moved quickly enough. Then he crept down the line of cars, checking the doors on each one.

"What are you doing?" Nia muttered.

Before he could answer, he found a car with the doors unlocked. Perfect.

"Go around," he told Nia quietly. "Get inside."

Her eyes widened. "Is this your car?"

"No. But you need to get in. We don't have time to talk right now." He climbed inside.

He began fiddling with the wires beneath the dash. Finally, Nia scrambled to the other door.

She rushed inside, a jumble of nerves with her jerky motions and shallow breathing. "You're seriously stealing this car? You don't think we have enough problems right now?"

He continued hotwiring the vehicle. "Unfortunately, neither of our vehicles are safe to drive."

"You mean—" Nia didn't finish her question, but the answer settled in her gaze.

With a pensive expression, she jerked her seatbelt across her chest. "I feel bad taking someone else's car."

"We'll return it. I know it's not ideal. But . . . there are no other options."

Finally, the sedan roared to life.

"Stay down low." Gage pulled on his own seatbelt and hit the accelerator.

He zipped down three levels of the parking garage, looking for any signs of those guys as he did.

So far, so good.

"I know what you did," Nia blurted beside him.

He craned his neck toward her, her words making no sense. "What?"

He turned toward the exit and waited for her to continue.

Her hand rested on her throat as if it had tightened. "You killed Rob."

Surprise jarred him. "I didn't kill Rob. *You* did."

Her eyes widened. "Why would *I* kill Rob?"

"That's an excellent question. I'd love to know that answer."

The two of them glanced at each other, questions floating between them.

What exactly was going on here?

Nia's heart pounded out of control as she stared at Gage.

He thought *she'd* killed Rob.

Why would he think that?

A chill swept over her.

Part of her knew she should run. Knew that jumping out of a moving vehicle was safer than going somewhere with Gage.

But another part felt frozen.

Still another part wanted to trust him—wanted to trust *someone*.

He'd kept her safe from the man trying to kill her.

But was that because he needed something from her?

As the sirens got louder, Gage turned to her. "Look, I didn't kill Rob. But if we don't get out of here soon, those guys are going to find us. When they do, they're going to kill both of us this time."

Her chill grew frostier. "Those guys? How many are there?"

"Two that I saw."

Nia stared at him a moment.

Although she had a million questions, she didn't voice any of them.

Not right now.

She wanted to look Gage in the eye when he answered.

Right now, she needed to let him drive.

"Stay low," he reminded her as he exited the garage and paused at the street.

Nia crouched in her seat, and Gage tugged his hat down.

Just as the police sped past, he turned right and peeled away from the parking garage.

Where was he taking her?

She wasn't sure she wanted to know.

"Take the battery out of your phone," he muttered as he accelerated in the opposite direction of the cops.

"What?" She stared at him, wondering why he'd tell her that.

"Just in case someone is tracking you."

She supposed that was a good point.

Reluctantly, she pulled out her phone and did as he asked. "What about you?"

"My phone is untraceable."

Her eyes narrowed with thought. "How do you have an untraceable phone?"

Gage didn't answer.

Nia remained lost in her thoughts as Gage continued to drive out of Miami, out of the suburbs, and away from any signs of life.

The lump in her throat grew larger. This was probably a bad idea.

She knew where this road led.

Gage was taking her to the Everglades, wasn't he?

The perfect place to dump a body.

Her body?

Maybe.

Nothing felt certain right now.

But Nia prayed she was doing the right thing.

chapter
twenty-five

GAGE FINALLY PULLED onto a side road, turned around, and backed the car up to a swampy area. He needed to see if anyone else came down this lane.

He'd kept his eyes on the dark road as he traveled, and he hadn't seen any headlights behind them. Unless these guys were tracking them another way—which Gage didn't think they were—he and Nia shouldn't be found.

All around them were miles of wetlands and a few scrubby trees. Their biggest danger should only be an alligator or two.

Being here should give them some time to talk.

Apparently, they had a lot of things to sort out.

Nia thought *he'd* killed Rob? Why would she think he'd killed his friend?

He was ready to get some answers.

He shifted toward her.

Before any questions left his lips, Nia faced him, fire flashing in her gaze. "Who are you? And don't lie to me."

"My name is Gage Pearson, just like I told you."

Her eyes narrowed. "But who are you really?"

"I told you."

She squinted, not bothering to hide her skepticism. "Who do you work for?"

"A computer company."

"What kind of computer company?" Agitation rose in her voice.

"Valid question . . ." he murmured. "We do computer security."

She continued to stare, and Gage gave her a moment to collect her thoughts. The woman was smart, and she didn't back down. Part of him admired that. The other part wished she would back off. It would make this much simpler.

Finally, Nia licked her lips and shifted. "Listen, I saw you in Rob's apartment. I was outside the building. I couldn't see your face very well, but I saw your tattoo. You killed him."

Wait . . . she'd seen him when he went to Rob's apartment?

There was a lot he wanted to ask about that.

If Nia had seen him early this morning in Rob's apartment, no wonder she thought he murdered Rob.

He raised his hands in the air. "I would never have hurt my friend. How in the world did you see me?"

Her jaw hardened. "That's not important."

Gage begged to differ.

"The truth is, I went to stay with him last night,"

Gage admitted. "But when I walked into his place, I found him dead already. I didn't kill him."

"Then why didn't you call the police?" Her voice cracked.

He bit down. "I did call them—anonymously. Now, why don't you tell me why *you* were in his apartment?"

Her face went pale. "How did you know that?"

"I saw the security footage."

Her eyes widened. "You're the one who erased it?"

"I didn't erase *you*." He reached into his pocket and pulled out something. "And I found this there. Look familiar?"

Nia stared at the earring and began to rub her temples. "I can explain."

Gage crossed his arms, curious about what kind of story she would come up with. This could be good. "I'm waiting."

Nia finished telling Gage the story and then studied his expression, determined to see if he believed her.

His arms remained crossed as he sat stiffly in the car. "So you're telling me that you told Rob good night after dinner, and you don't remember anything else until you woke up beside his dead body?"

"I know how it sounds." Nia's voice pitched with nerves, and she tried to calm herself. The task felt useless. "I really do. When I woke up and saw he was dead, I panicked. I knew how it would look. So I ran."

"But you didn't *just* run. You cleaned up part of the crime scene first, didn't you?"

Nausea rose in her as memories flashed back to her. "I *did* try to conceal any evidence I'd been there. Only because I was freaking out. I've never been in a situation like that, and I didn't know what to do."

He stared at her.

"The killer was in the apartment with me. Took a photo of me beside Rob's dead body. Texted it to me and said if I didn't follow his instructions, he'd send the picture to the police."

Gage's eyes widened. "What does he want from you?"

She shook her head. "That's the thing. I don't know yet. I'm still waiting."

Silence passed, and Nia waited to hear if Gage believed her or not.

After several minutes, he squinted skeptically. "Why can't you remember?"

Nia shrugged then shook her head slowly as she wrestled with her thoughts. "I have no idea. I'm shaken by this whole thing also. If we don't find the killer, then I'm most likely to take the fall for this."

Gage continued to study her as if trying to figure out if he believed anything she said.

But she wasn't the only one hiding something right now. Gage had his own secrets. That was clear.

Her gaze locked with his. "Now are you finally going to tell me the truth also?"

Nia waited to hear what he had to say.

Would he tell her the truth? Or would he feed her more lies?

His next move would determine whether or not Nia could trust him.

And if she couldn't trust him, that meant she was out here in the middle of nowhere with a man who screamed danger.

chapter
twenty-six

GAGE STARED at the vast nothingness in front of him and contemplated what to say to Nia.

He couldn't share too much. He was bound by contract to remain quiet about the intricacies of his job. About his past military career. Things were on a need-to-know basis.

Did Nia really need to know any of this?

Yet if he wanted to figure out what happened to his friend, he would need to explain something. To offer some hint of the truth, at least.

He blew out a long breath before saying, "I work for a private security group. And I honestly did come here to visit my friend after he called me. That's all true."

Nia narrowed her eyes as if not ready to believe him yet. "What kind of private security group is this that you work for? You seem to know what you're doing when it comes to evading the gunmen."

"I'm former military—that's how I know some of the things I do. I use that experience in my current job."

"What kind of 'jobs' do you do usually? I feel like you're beating around the bush."

That was because he was. "Things other people don't want to do. Things I can't get caught doing. Things that require a high level of both expertise and innovative technologies."

She smirked. "So you're not just a computer repair guy?"

He shrugged. "I mean, I *can* work on computers. But I use that cover story because I can't afford to go around telling everyone what I really do. It's too risky."

"But your name really is Gage?"

"It is."

"And you're really from Kansas?"

He didn't say anything. Didn't tell her he'd grown up in Michigan.

After a moment, Nia nodded with resignation. "Okay, I guess I can understand if you need to keep that quiet . . ."

"I'm not here to hurt you, Nia," Gage said. "I'm here to help my friend. I need to find out what happened to him."

She studied him another moment before nodding slowly, almost reluctantly. "I guess that makes sense. Thank you for sharing."

"Of course."

She scanned everything around them, and Gage

followed her gaze. Even though it was growing darker by the moment, she could still see the reeds blowing gently with the wind. Shrubby trees rose from the otherwise flatness of the wetlands. Somewhere in the distance, the hum of an airboat could barely be heard.

"What now?" Nia crossed her arms, unmistakable tension surrounding her.

"I think we go back to the hotel and recalculate—after we ditch this car."

"Is it safe to go back?"

Gage thought about it before nodding. "We'll be careful."

Nia slowly nodded before she drew in a breath and said, "Okay, then. Let's go recalculate and figure out what's really going on."

Nia's thoughts were still racing after she and Gage had ditched the car they'd "borrowed," as Gage had said.

They stepped inside the Royal Oasis and waited for the elevator.

So far, so good. She hadn't seen signs anyone was following them. Based on Gage's body language, he hadn't seen anyone either.

With any luck, they'd make it back to the room without any incidents.

She could hope, at least.

Gage was full of surprises.

She sensed he was telling the truth back in the Glades. His story . . . it was wild. She tried to imagine his past and how that had shaped him into the person he was today. She couldn't begin to understand it.

Did he believe what Nia had told him? She wasn't sure. But it had felt good to get it off her chest.

The elevator dinged, and they stepped inside.

No one else was with them.

Another good thing.

But she knew they were far from being out of trouble.

There was still so much they needed to figure out.

And at the top of her list? Uncovering what had happened to her memories.

She kept hoping something would resurface and give her a clue about last night.

But so far, her thoughts were blank. She still had no idea what had happened or why she'd forgotten.

Being drugged made the most sense. It just seemed strange that once the drugs had worn off, she still couldn't remember.

It was unnerving, really.

But maybe—just maybe—she really could trust Gage. It would be nice to have someone on her side. To not go through this investigation alone.

The elevator stopped, the doors opened, and they padded down the expensive carpet toward their suite.

Gage unlocked the door and pushed it open.

But as soon as Nia stepped inside, she saw a man standing there.

A broad man with a hulking build and sharp eyes.

Eyes that stared at them without even a hint of fear.

She took a step back, her lungs tightening so quickly she could barely breathe.

Was this the man who'd chased her? If so, how had he found her here?

chapter
twenty-seven

GAGE SAW Nia's reaction and placed a hand on her arm. "It's okay. It's just my colleague."

Her shoulders fell as she let out a breath. "I thought . . ."

He squeezed her bicep. "I know. I'm sorry. I should have mentioned he was here."

Austin stepped toward them just then, his arm outstretched. "Austin Greenwich. Sorry to scare you."

Nia studied him a moment, took in his short beard, his broad shoulders, his brooding gaze. Then she extended her arm and shook his hand. "Nia Anderson."

Gage double-checked the locks on the door before turning back to his colleague. "Have you been back long?"

"Ten minutes. Everything okay with you guys?" Austin glanced back and forth between them.

Gage stole another glance at Nia, remembering their

earlier conversation, before nodding. "We had a rough go of it for a while, but we're back here now, and we're fine. Why don't we all sit down?"

He strode toward the couch, Nia and Austin following.

"I'd offer you something to drink or eat," Gage started. "But all I have is what's here in the hotel room."

"I already ordered a pizza." Austin offered a goofy grin. "It should be here any minute. Splurged and got some soda and a cookie pizza to go with it too."

The man was fit and muscular. But no one should ever stand in the way of Austin and food.

"Perfect." Gage sat on the couch but didn't relax.

His thoughts still raced too fast. He had too much on his mind. Too many questions about Rob. About what Nia had told him.

He glanced at Nia as she gingerly lowered herself onto the couch. Questions brewed in her gaze, and Gage knew she was uncomfortable with Austin's presence here. He needed to set her at ease.

"Austin and I work together, and I asked him to check out a few things for us," Gage explained.

"A few things like what?" She rubbed her arms as if chilled.

"I checked out Brittany and Cormac." Austin sat in a seat adjacent to them.

"And?" Gage asked.

"Brittany was out with her friends partying, just like you said."

Nia's gaze swerved toward Gage. "How did you know she was out partying?"

He filled her in on the conversation with Brittany's mom.

At that update, Nia let out a quick puff of air. "Why would Brittany say she and Rob were dating and act so upset that he'd been killed if they hadn't even dated that long and weren't even still together?"

"That's what we need to figure out."

"I looked into Cormac also," Austin said. "He's not at his house."

"I heard he was on a trip," Nia said.

"That's where this gets a little weird." Austin shifted. "A neighbor said that he saw Cormac yesterday. He was acting strange. Came out from his house with a bag, glancing around everywhere like he was looking for someone."

"So the neighbor talked to him?" Gage asked.

"Yeah, he said something like, where's the fire? Cormac tried to laugh it off. Said he was late for a meeting and that's why he was in such a hurry. But if you ask me, it sounds suspicious."

"Considering everything that has happened, it sounds suspicious to me also," Gage said. "We need to figure out where he went because he might just have the answers we need."

～

The pizza came a moment later. Nia grabbed a piece as she shared what she'd learned.

She wasn't hungry but nibbled on a piece of pepperoni then sipped on a bottle of water that cost almost as much as an entire meal.

Then she told Gage and Austin about how she'd used a program her company had to search Rob's phone records. She shared the printouts with the unknown caller's number. Pointed out Cormac's number. Hector's number. Gage's number.

Nia couldn't be sure, but she thought she saw a spark of admiration in Gage's gaze. He hadn't expected her to take such a risk, had he?

She'd always liked surprising people.

Kind of like when she'd started her business in a male-dominated tech world. She'd gotten lots of skeptical looks. So many people had doubted her.

But she'd been determined to succeed anyway.

Now those very same people came to her asking for advice. One had even asked for a job.

Throughout that whole process, Nia had tried to learn to be gracious.

Grace was something she needed in her own life, so it seemed as if she should offer grace to others as well.

Including Gage.

Even though the man hadn't been totally honest with her, she hadn't been totally honest with him either. They were both dealing with a murder, and doing the best they could to muddle through it.

She placed her half-eaten slice on the box top of the pizza and then wiped her mouth with a napkin.

"What do we do next?" Nia asked. "If we don't find this killer, I'm afraid I'll go to prison for this. It's only a matter of time before the police discover I was in his apartment. I know how this looks."

It looked like she was the killer.

chapter
twenty-eight

"WE NEED TO DEVELOP A PLAN," Gage said, purposefully shifting the conversation. "One of our first orders of business should be figuring out why you've lost your memory, Nia."

Of all the things she'd expected him to say, that probably hadn't been one of them. But he couldn't stop thinking about it. They needed to find some answers.

Nia pulled her legs beneath her and sank deeper into the chair. "I keep thinking about it, and I just don't know."

"No tenderness on your head from where you could have been hit?" Austin grabbed another piece of pizza.

"No." Nia touched the side of her head as if feeling again for bumps or sore spots. "It was one of the first things I thought about."

"No needle marks on your arms or anywhere else?" Gage asked.

"I thought there was a spot on my arm at first, but I

think it was just a mosquito bite." She paused. "I suppose something could have been slipped into my drink. But, at this point, I'm not sure how much good it would do to go to the hospital and be tested. The risk may not be worth the reward. It would take a lot of time to get the results."

"I'm not sure what else it could be if it wasn't a drug," Gage said. "Let's say something was put in your drink. Did you walk away from the table during dinner?"

Nia shook her head. "I didn't. Rob and I met for a couple of hours, and the conversation was pretty intense. There were no opportunities to get up."

"You don't think that Rob . . . ?" Austin didn't finish his question.

Gage swung his head back and forth. "He wouldn't have put a drug into her drink. I know him. He wouldn't do that."

"I can't see him doing that either. But unless the waiter did it . . . I don't know how it would have gotten there. I suppose someone who's amazing with sleight of hand tricks could have walked past." She frowned. "But Rob and I were sitting against the wall, and I just can't see it happening."

Gage's thoughts still raced. He didn't have any other good explanations as to what could have happened.

The last thing Nia remembered was being in that restaurant, so something had clearly occurred after their meal.

They needed to retrace the timeline. They'd find some answers if they did.

"You said the conversation was intense." Gage shifted in his seat. "Did Rob give you any clues about why he wanted to back out of the contract? Have you remembered anything new?"

Nia stared off in the distance, her eyes darting back and forth as if she tried to recall something. "Rob just told me he thought he could improve on the project and that it wasn't ready for release. I pressed him to go deeper with that. I'd seen the app myself and thought it was great. Honestly, when he told me that, I thought he was being too hard on himself. That's why I didn't capitulate to what he was saying."

"So you weren't going to let him back out of the contract?" Gage clarified.

"It wasn't as simple as that." Nia ran a hand through her hair, leaving her curls standing on end. "We had signed a legally binding contract. This wasn't something that just popped up in a day after we signed the paperwork. This deal has been in the works for months. Up until yesterday, Rob was excited about it."

"So this goes back to the fact that something happened between his meeting in your office and the time that he called and asked you to meet him for dinner . . ." Gage wished he had some type of magic device that would let him see into the past. If only those existed.

"Someone texted him right as he was leaving my office. Then he had a call from that same number twenty minutes later," Nia noted. "My best guess is that phone call was what set this in motion. If we could figure out who made the call, then maybe we could get some answers. But like I said, the call came from a burner."

"Do we know if Rob went back to his apartment in between going to your office and meeting you that night?" Austin took a long swig of Mountain Dew as he waited for their answer.

"We don't know for sure," Nia said.

"We could try to track down the security footage to show him from the time he left and see where he went after that," Gage said. "It's going to take work. We're going to have to pinpoint every camera between there and his apartment and see what happened."

Nia sat up straighter. "If we could do something like that, then we could also see what happened between the time at the restaurant and the time I got to Rob's apartment. Maybe that could provide us with some answers as well."

Gage glanced at Austin. "Do you think you could work on that for us?"

"Absolutely." Austin nodded.

"What are we going to do?" Nia turned back to Gage. "I know it's late. But I don't want to just sit here and twiddle my thumbs."

"Maybe we should try to track down Brittany," Gage suggested. "She did ask for my help. And her actions all seem pretty suspicious, wouldn't you say?"

"I would," Nia agreed.

Gage glanced back at Austin. "Where did you say you saw her again?"

"She was at a place called Avenue 12."

"Why in the world would Brittany go back to Avenue 12?" Nia asked as she and Gage left the hotel room.

"That's an excellent question," Gage said. "Something we're going to need to figure out."

Austin had given her a new phone since Nia's had been disabled. This one was untraceable, and she'd routed her old number to it. Gage had insisted that it was only safe she had a cell in case something went wrong.

She agreed.

Nia glanced at her outfit. She'd cleaned the smudges from her face, but her clothes were a different story. They still looked dirty.

"I don't think I'll be allowed into the club wearing this." Then she shot a glance at him. "You either—no offense."

"No offense taken. Let's see if the boutique downstairs is still open. We might have a few minutes until it closes if we're lucky. I know they sell some high-end clothes in there."

Just as they got downstairs, an unsmiling middle-aged brunette pulled metal gates over the opening of the clothing store.

Gage strode up to the woman and plastered on an apologetic smile. "I know you're closing, and I hate to ask you this. But is there any chance my girlfriend and I can grab new outfits? We lost our luggage, and we really want to go out tonight. I promise we'll be quick."

An annoyed expression crossed her face, and she

continued to tug the gate over the storefront. "I'm getting ready to leave."

"I know, and that's why I hate to ask. But what if we only took five minutes of your time? We flew all the way here from Des Moines, and we certainly didn't come here so we could stay in the hotel all night."

The woman's eyes flickered back and forth between the two of them. Her gaze assessed the smudges on their clothes from being underneath that car, and she sneered.

"You certainly can't go out on the town looking like you do." She paused and let out a breath through her nose. Then she nodded and sighed. "Five minutes. That's all I'm giving you. Please don't make me regret this. My daughter has a band concert tonight."

"We'll make it worth your time," Gage promised. "And you won't be late. I don't want that on my shoulders."

She stepped aside, and Nia and Gage rushed inside.

"Find something understated," Gage whispered as they wove between clothing racks. "We need to stay below the radar."

Those had been Nia's thoughts also.

She scrambled around, looking for something she could wear that would be a sure fit. She knew she didn't have time to try anything on. She found a black bodycon-style dress in her size, as well as a pair of strappy black sandals and a wristlet.

They would have to do.

Besides, black would help her to blend in, and the stretchy fabric would be comfortable.

Gage had already grabbed something as well, and they checked out.

Then Gage flashed another smile at the snooty employee as he slipped her a couple extra bills, and the woman's shoulders relaxed some.

Was Gage one of those guys? The kind who could charm people?

Nia had a feeling the answer was yes. However, he also had a sincerity about him that confused her. He was suspicious yet concerned. Accusatory but protective.

Who was Gage Pearson? Who was he really?

They slipped back into the lobby and disappeared into their respective bathrooms to get cleaned up and changed.

After Nia put on the dress, she stared at herself in the mirror. It would be better if she had some makeup to touch up her face. But, overall, she looked much better—and much more appropriate for going out tonight.

Now she only hoped that Gage approved.

chapter
twenty-nine

GAGE SAW Nia step out from the bathroom, and his eyes widened.

He let out a low whistle.

It was quite the transformation. She'd looked beautiful before while wearing her business casual.

Right now, she simply looked stunning.

The dress fit her perfectly and showed off every curve. Her hair looked full and her curls bouncy. He'd said they needed to be understated, but Gage knew that was nearly impossible for someone like Nia. She had a natural beauty that radiated from her.

She glanced at him almost nervously. "Am I okay?"

"You're more than okay. You look great."

A smile drifted across her lips. "Thanks. You look nice too."

He glanced down at the white designer jeans he'd bought, along with a black button-up shirt and black dress shoes.

Then he offered his arm. "You ready for this?"

She nodded. "I am. I'm ready to find answers."

"We stick together," he reminded her.

Gage had his gun with him, but he doubted he could get it past security at the club. He'd leave it locked in the car instead. He'd already set it up to use the Porsche again, just to be on the safe side.

He knew how to handle himself in these situations. But it made him nervous thinking about bringing Nia with him. There was a possibility they could get themselves into some sticky situations.

Yet he knew she wouldn't have it any other way.

Besides, if she saw someone or heard something, it might bring back some memories. If Nia could remember what had happened . . . then maybe they'd find the answers they needed.

Nia brushed off her nerves as she and Gage parked on the street a block away from Avenue 12.

She hadn't expected to come back here, yet here she was.

After climbing out, she took Gage's arm so they could look as if they were a couple.

A long line stretched along the sidewalk outside the club.

Waiting in that would take up a lot of their valuable time.

Gage seemed to read her thoughts and strode to the front of the line.

Cal, the bouncer from earlier, stood there and recognized them right away. "You two again? Think you can get a special favor just because you talked to the boss earlier?"

"As a potential investor, I need to check this place out so I can understand the vibe," Nia said.

The man stared at her and grunted, unconvinced.

She stepped closer. "And you know . . . when I have a say-so in operations around here, I plan to give everyone a raise. Cost of living has gone up, and employees deserve to be better compensated. The boss shouldn't be filthy rich while his employees are barely scraping by."

Something flashed in his eyes. Then he nodded and stepped back.

Relief washed through Nia, but she maintained her composure.

Her ruse had worked.

Cal moved to the side and let them in.

She released the air from her lungs and held onto Gage's arm tighter.

"Good job," he whispered as they paused on the other side of the doorway.

"Thanks."

"Now we need to find Brittany."

They scanned the massive club. The place was packed —with probably two hundred people at least. The dance floor was crowded with people swaying and bobbing to loud music. Lights flashed overhead.

It would be hard to find anyone in this place.

"We could split up," Nia said the words loudly in order to be heard over the music.

Gage's jaw tightened as he shook his head. "Bad idea. We stick together. No matter what."

Nia knew he'd mentioned that in the car, but she wondered if he might change his mind.

He didn't. That was fine because being with him did make her feel a little safer.

She studied the sea of people in front of her, glad she wasn't in this scene anymore. It had seemed like so much fun at the time. But looking back, those days had left her with a sense of emptiness.

Now, she'd much rather stay in for the night, play a board game, and have a nice dinner.

Things could change in such a short amount of time.

Just then, a familiar face caught her eye.

But it wasn't Brittany that captured her attention.

chapter
thirty

AS GAGE STUDIED THE CROWD, Nia grabbed his arm and pointed to someone across the room.

"I can't be certain," she muttered, "but isn't that . . . Cormac?"

Gage had only seen the guy's picture on social media, but he was hard to miss with his fiery red hair and six-foot-five build.

That man *did* look like Cormac. But the guy they watched didn't seem to be here for fun. Based on the way he weaved through the crowd, he was searching for someone.

And Cormac—if that was him—was supposed to be out of town.

So what was he doing here at Avenue 12?

Gage took Nia's hand. "Let's go find out why he's here."

His eyes still on Cormac, he moved through the

crowd, winding between people dancing to robotic, pulsating music.

They reached the other side of the club and paused.

Where had Cormac gone?

A group of people had moved in front of Gage and Nia, dancing obnoxiously, and he'd taken his eyes off Cormac only for a few seconds.

In that amount of time, the guy had disappeared.

"He can't be too far away," Nia said above the music.

She was right. But . . .

A huge bar lined with stools stretched against the far wall, and an alcove leading into the bathrooms wasn't terribly far away.

Could Cormac have picked up his pace and gone that way?

There was only one way to find out.

Gage led Nia toward the bathrooms. They seemed like the best bet. Unless Cormac had ducked behind the bar, there was nowhere else for him to hide.

They reached a short, dark hallway.

Several people lingered in the space . . . but no Cormac.

Gage would check inside, but that would require leaving Nia out here alone.

That wasn't what he wanted to do.

Instead, they could wait for a few minutes.

But Gage's suspicions about the man continued to rise.

They *definitely* needed to talk to him.

Gage stood to the side with Nia as the minutes ticked by.

Cormac didn't emerge from the bathroom.

Other men had come and gone.

Maybe Cormac wasn't there.

"Do you think he saw us and slipped away?" Nia looked up, her eyes widening as if she hadn't expected him to be so close.

His throat went dry as he stared into her eyes. As an unexpected flash of desire pulsed through him.

He wondered what it would be like to kiss her. To lean down. To press his lips onto hers.

The impulse was startling. He'd been trained to remain focused at all times. To resign himself to a life of singleness.

So why were these feelings rearing up now?

He swallowed hard and remembered her question. *Do you think he saw us and slipped away?*

Gage knew it was a possibility.

But if Cormac had done that, that definitely meant he was hiding something.

Nia didn't know how they'd lost Cormac.

It was almost as if he'd disappeared into thin air—which clearly wasn't a possibility.

But if he wasn't down this hallway, that meant he'd probably headed to the bar.

Maybe he'd ducked behind it, trying to throw them off his trail.

They didn't come all the way out here just to be waylaid again.

Could Cormac still be here?

Gage seemed to be on the same wavelength as she was. Still holding her hand, he pulled her back toward the dance floor. She tried to ignore how nice his hand felt against hers. Tried to ignore how much she liked the calloused toughness of his palms. To ignore the strength in his grasp.

Midway across the dance floor, they nearly collided with someone.

Nia sucked in a breath when she saw the face in front of her. "Brittany?"

Brittany stared at her, her eyes orbs of confusion. The woman wore a nearly nonexistent beige dress. Seriously, Nia had seen bikinis that covered more skin. The woman's hair flowed around her shoulders in oversized curls and black mascara framed her eyes.

As she glanced at Gage, recognition filled her expression. "Gage? I didn't expect to see you here."

Gage remained standoffish—probably remembering the way the woman had clung to him earlier. "You're actually just the person we were hoping to talk to."

chapter
thirty-one

BRITTANY LED Gage and Nia out the back exit and into a small alley behind the club. She placed a brick in the doorway to keep the door from closing and locking them out.

The woman didn't look nearly as perky now as she had when she'd run into them outside Rob's apartment, Gage mused.

Was she trying to fake her grief? Or was she simply upset because Gage and Nia had found her here?

"Any luck figuring out what happened to Rob?" Brittany's voice sounded softer than it had inside the club as she turned to them.

"We've been trying to find answers," Gage told her. "We're hoping you might have some information that could help us."

She pointed to herself. "Me? You think I have answers?"

"I actually talked to someone who told me the two of you broke up." Gage watched her expression, interested to see how she would react.

"Broke up?" She nearly snorted. "Who told you that? You know what, it doesn't matter. I could see why someone would be confused."

"Could you explain that?" Nia asked.

"I mean, I guess Rob did *officially* break up with me." She rolled her eyes. "But I knew it was only temporary. He was totally into me, and we were going to get back together. He just needed some time."

Her expression drooped as if she remembered that time was something they didn't have anymore.

"Why were you so certain that you were going to get back together?" Nia asked.

"I think Rob really liked me. And I liked him too. We had a good time together, and I think he just got cold feet. He told me he didn't like to casually date. But I wasn't sure he was ready to jump into something serious either."

Brittany was totally clueless. Gage had no doubt about that. The woman didn't appear to give any deep reflective thought to anything.

"And you'd only been together for two weeks?" Gage continued to press.

"Yeah, but when you know, you know." She crossed her arms. "And why are you questioning me about this? *I* didn't kill him."

"You said you thought Darius might have had him killed," Nia reminded her.

If the woman thought Darius was a killer, why would she be here at his club tonight? It didn't make sense. Not to Gage.

Brittany frowned. "I just figured since now that things were over between me and Rob that maybe . . ."

"And by things being over you mean now that Rob's dead?" Gage's tone contained an edge of disgust.

Brittany sighed, puckering her lips into an overblown frown. "Look, I'm not used to being single. And I thought maybe Darius wanted another chance."

"But didn't you cheat on him?" Nia clarified.

Brittany rolled her eyes. "It's confusing."

"Then why don't you explain it for us?" Gage prodded.

Then they waited to hear what she had to say.

Nia watched Brittany, having trouble taking her seriously.

Nia had met Brittany's type before. The beautiful but insecure type who always needed a man on her arm or she didn't know what to do with herself.

Based on what Gage had said earlier, Brittany was the kind of woman who probably looked for a man who could support her lifestyle so she didn't have to work.

Just like her mom was supporting her lifestyle now.

The shallowness of it didn't impress Nia. But she tried not to be too judgmental.

However, there was still the possibility Brittany knew more than she was letting on about Rob's death.

"I told Rob when we met that I'd broken up with Darius when I hadn't actually broken up with him yet," Brittany said. "So Rob didn't really know the whole truth."

"But you didn't tell Darius that?" Gage asked.

She shrugged. "It didn't matter. He wouldn't listen to me anyway. He's the jealous type, despite what he might have told you."

Nia could see Darius as being more territorial than jealous. Losing a girlfriend to another man probably wounded his pride or made him feel inferior.

"Listen, Brittany," Nia started. "You need to tell it to us straight. Do you really think that Darius did something to Rob? Because that wasn't the sense I got from him."

She sighed and glanced to the side.

Trying to come up with a cover story, if Nia had to guess. Brittany hadn't expected all these questions to be directed at her.

"Just tell us the truth." Gage lowered his voice. "If you really want to know what happened to Rob, then stop leading us on these wild goose chases."

She sighed and rolled her eyes again. "The truth is, I *did* wonder if Darius could have done something like this. But after talking to him today and seeing how uninterested he was, it made me question my initial reaction. Darius really doesn't want anything to do with me. In fact, I think he's already dating someone else." Red crept up Brittany's neck as if that embarrassed her.

Nia figured Brittany had tried to woo Darius back, despite the fact he was dating someone else, and he'd rejected her. That had probably injured her delicate ego.

In that sense, Brittany and Darius had probably been perfect for each other.

"If all that is true . . ." Gage twisted his neck, waiting for Brittany to finish.

"It is," Brittany interjected, nodding with exuberance. "I promise."

"If that is true," he repeated, "then who might have killed Rob? In the two weeks that you dated, did you notice anything strange that might help us figure that out?"

She crossed her arms in front of her and let out another sigh. "I know he was really excited about that app he'd developed. Every time I went over, he was trying to tweak it. He just wanted it to be perfect."

"And?" Nia waited for her to continue.

"There's nothing weird I could see about it. The only thing I know is I came over one time after he'd been playing with it, and he had a strange expression on his face. I asked him what was wrong, but he wouldn't tell me anything. I figured maybe he'd discovered a bug in his app or found some type of problem he couldn't fix. You know Rob. He always wanted things done right. It was one of the things I liked about him."

Nia stared at the woman.

Initially, she'd wondered if Brittany had something to

do with his death. But now she didn't think so. The woman wasn't smart enough to pull it off—even if she had help from someone else.

But if Brittany wasn't the killer, and Darius wasn't the killer . . . that really meant that they needed to find Cormac.

chapter
thirty-two

AFTER BRITTANY WENT BACK INSIDE, Gage made sure the brick still kept the door open so he and Nia could also slip back in when they were ready. But it would be easier to talk out here than inside.

He turned to Nia. She'd done a fantastic job questioning Brittany. She almost seemed like a natural, an expert at reading people.

He'd been impressed.

For a moment, he'd thought about recommending her for a job at the Shadow Agency.

Then he realized he'd never put her through that.

Living the way he did wasn't easy. Always on the go. Never knowing the assignment. Sometimes arguing about the ethics of what they'd been asked to do.

The truth was that he'd had memory lapses before also. That he had scars from the experiments done on him. That he wondered if there was more to his time being a military lab rat than he ever realized.

He'd been programmed for a solitary life. Yet the essence of who he was and what he'd wanted had never gone away. It had just been shoved to the recesses of his mind.

"What do you think?" Gage studied her face.

Nia shook her head, a weary look in her gaze. "I think that woman is a hot mess. But I don't think she's a killer."

"I don't think so either. And I honestly don't think that Darius is involved with this either." Gage paused. "But what about what she said concerning Rob looking upset that one time? Any idea what that could have been about?"

Nia shook her head. "He was a perfectionist. If he found anything wrong with his app it would have upset him. But he never mentioned anything to me up until our dinner last night. Even then, he still didn't give me any details."

"Is there anyone else you know of whom Rob might have talked to about the app? Who could have given him feedback on it?"

"Cormac is the only person I can think of." Nia shrugged almost apologetically.

"We really need to find this guy."

"Yes, we do."

"Let's give it another shot." Gage opened the door and the two of them walked inside.

But as soon as they reached the dance floor, a bullet sliced the air, cutting through the sound of the loud, pulsating music.

Nia's heart ratcheted with fear.

There was a gunman.

Inside the club.

Gage grabbed her hand and jerked her to the floor behind a table.

Then he looked up, searching for the gunman.

But chaos erupted as people ran for their lives and tried to escape.

As the dance floor cleared, one person remained.

Lying on the floor.

With blood on his or her chest.

Nia raised her head, desperate to see who'd been hurt. But she was too far away to make out any details. Too many people were around.

"It's Darius," Gage muttered.

Fear rocked through her.

Who would have shot Darius?

It couldn't have been Brittany. She wouldn't have had time. And Nia didn't think she had it in her to do something like this.

But there was always Cormac. Could he be the one behind this?

Even more . . . was he here somewhere, lurking in the shadows?

chapter
thirty-three

DARIUS HAD BEEN SHOT.

Gage stared at his body in the middle of the floor. He wanted to rush toward the man. To take over the investigation.

But two security guards sprinted to Darius's side. One stripped off his shirt and put it over the wound on the man's chest to stop the blood flow. The other had a walkie-talkie to his mouth.

Brittany rushed toward Darius, sobs escaping as her arms flailed. One of the security guards lifted his arm to hold her back.

It appeared Darius was still alive.

For now.

But who had done this to him?

Gage scanned the people still in the club.

But he didn't see a gunman.

Had the man run?

That was the most likely thing. With all the people in

here and the darkness, the man could have easily been obscured.

What about Cormac?

Gage glanced around, but he didn't see the man anywhere.

Nia still trembled beneath his fingers.

He should probably get her out of here.

But before he could tug her toward the door, police invaded the place.

As police swarmed the place, Nia's phone buzzed.

> Give us all the paperwork you have from Rob Lesner.

She swallowed hard. *That* was what these people wanted?

She sucked in a shallow breath before responding.

> I can't do that.

A couple of seconds passed before the sender responded again.

> I'll send that picture to the police.

This person was trying to manipulate her. Nia couldn't let that happen.

If she let them get away with this, what else would they demand in the future?

If they sent that picture to the police, she'd simply have to tell the cops the truth.

It would be painful. Hard.

The action could change the course of her life.

But she couldn't let this go on.

With trembling hands, she responded.

> Then send the photo to the cops.

Nausea filled her as soon as she hit Send, but she knew it had been the right choice.

"Everything okay?" Gage peered at her phone.

Nia showed him the texts, and his eyes widened. "Are you sure that's what you want to say?"

She frowned but nodded. "Unfortunately, it's the only way. I'm not going to let this person—or these people—intimidate me."

Gage's neck twisted in surprise. "I can appreciate that . . . but I hope you don't regret it."

Her hands trembled as she put her phone back into her wristlet.

She and Gage were trapped here now that police had surrounded all the exits.

Part of her wanted to stay, to see if she could find out more information.

The other part of her wanted to run, to hide.

Instead, she did what she often did when in fear: she froze.

Stood there.

Unmoving.

Not saying a word.

Only thinking.

She didn't know who to trust. Didn't know if one of the men who'd been following her earlier might be in this room now. Might be watching her.

At least Gage stood beside her. He seemed well-equipped. She'd found an unusual comfort when he held her hand. When he'd used his own body to shield her when he'd heard that gunfire.

The act hadn't gone unnoticed.

The police were already going around and beginning to question people. Paramedics were working on Darius.

Thank goodness, he was still alive.

Nia wasn't sure what part, if any, he might have played in Rob's death. But seeing the man like this . . . she didn't wish that on anyone.

"Just stay cool," Gage whispered.

She nodded, trying to keep her racing heart under control.

Across the room, Nia saw Brittany crying, her face in her hands. Nia should go comfort the woman. Even if Brittany was shallow and flighty, she still appeared to be honestly grieving.

"First Rob and now Darius?" Gage whispered.

"I know. Is there a connection?"

Gage frowned. "It seems as if there might be. And that connection could be Brittany."

She swallowed hard, unable to deny his words.

A cop approached just then and said he needed to ask them some questions.

Nia pulled her gaze from Brittany. Maybe she'd talk to the woman later.

Before the cop could ask them anything, the door at the front entrance opened, and a man stepped inside.

Nia sucked in a breath.

Mario.

She hadn't seen him in nearly two years.

But now he was right here.

At Avenue 12.

His gaze met hers, and something flickered there.

It almost looked like . . . satisfaction. Like he'd been waiting for the opportunity to question her. To put her in the hot seat.

That sounded about right.

"Nia?" Gage asked beside her.

She pulled her gaze away from Mario. "Yes?"

"Is everything okay? You flinched."

"Did I?" Her voice sounded thin.

"Most definitely."

She glanced back over at Mario and saw him heading their way.

chapter
thirty-four

GAGE WATCHED the man walking toward them.

Was this guy the reason Nia was so shaken? What sense would that make? It wasn't as if Nia had ever been on the wrong side of the law. But that detective they'd run into earlier had also seemed to make her off-balance.

There was clearly a story here.

The man didn't bother to introduce himself. Instead, he went straight to Nia and paused in front of her—standing a little too close. At least from Gage's perspective.

The guy dismissed the cop taking their statement.

His eyes remained on Nia, an almost possessive look to them. "Long time no see."

Nia raised her chin, her body still tense. "It's been a while."

"This isn't the type of establishment I thought you would frequent." His gaze quickly scanned the place.

Nia shrugged, almost unnaturally calm. "Trying something different."

The man's gaze flickered to Gage, and he lifted his chin in a stiff nod. "Police Chief Mario Cruz."

"Gage Pearson," he responded with an equal amount of standoffishness.

Gage didn't know why, but he didn't like this guy or the vibes he gave off.

"Did you see anything that might help us identify the shooter?" the chief asked.

"I heard the gunshot, and then it was chaos as everybody started to run," Nia said. "I glanced around, trying to figure out what exactly had happened, but I didn't see anything."

Cruz turned to Gage. "And you?"

"The same," Gage said. "It was chaos in here. But I didn't see the shooter."

Cruz studied Gage another uncomfortable moment. "You from around here?"

Gage shook his head. "Wichita."

"And what brings you to Miami?"

"A friend asked me to come and visit, and so I did."

The chief's eyes seemed to be calculating something, and then he let out a grunt. "You're Rob Lesner's friend, aren't you?"

"I am."

"So you come to town, and Rob dies, and now you're here, and Darius is shot?"

Gage bristled. "Are you trying to imply something?"

"Just an observation." Lasers seemed to shoot from the chief's eyes.

"It sounded a little bit like an accusation," Gage shot back.

The chief's eyes narrowed as if he didn't like that response. Then he looked back at Nia. "And how do the two of you know each other?"

Gage wanted to tell the man it was none of his business. But he'd already gotten on the chief's bad side, and he knew he should back off. For Nia's sake.

"We met because of Rob," Nia answered, her voice light but distant. "We were both shocked to learn what had happened to him."

"So shocked that the two of you decided to hang out and come to a nightclub together?"

Gage could see where their presence here could look suspicious. But he didn't want the chief to know they were looking into Rob's death. There was no need to put that information out there. It wouldn't help the situation any.

"I guess you don't know who did this?" Nia expertly maneuvered around the chief's question.

"We're trying to figure it out. But we think it may have been this guy." Cruz pulled out his phone and held up a picture.

Gage's eyes widened when he saw a photo of . . . Cormac.

∾

Before Nia realized her reaction, she sucked in her breath.

She couldn't believe Cormac's face was there.

She thought the man might be up to something. But shooting Darius and running?

That hadn't been on her radar.

The man had seemed nice enough when she'd talked to him in the past.

"I guess you know him?" Mario stared at Nia as if trying to catch her in a lie.

She hated that condescending tone in his voice. Hated the way he looked down on her. Hated the way he lied.

But right now, she needed to remain composed. The last thing she wanted to do was to show any weakness around him. Mario would only exploit it if she did.

"Cormac worked with Rob," she said. "I didn't know the man personally, but I've heard Rob talk about him. I did meet him briefly once."

Mario grunted. "What exactly did Rob say about him?"

"Not much, like I said." Nia shrugged. "They seemed to like hanging out with each other. And Cormac was more the business side of things whereas Rob was the creative side. I did hear . . ."

She paused and wondered how much she should say.

"What did you hear?" Mario asked.

Nia licked her lips before saying, "I did hear Cormac was out of town. As you can imagine, I'm surprised to hear you think he did this."

"Who told you he was out of town?"

"I believe Rob may have mentioned it in one of our conversations. Either way, I haven't seen him around since Rob died so I just assumed that was accurate." Nia narrowed her gaze with confusion. "But why would Cormac do this?"

"Knowing Darius?" Mario gave a pointed look. "Probably drugs."

Nia was surprised Mario had admitted that much. But it sounded like Darius might have a pretty regular relationship with the police.

It wouldn't surprise her if someone like Darius was into drugs either. He gave off those vibes.

Mario looked at them both again before stepping back. "I'll be in touch if I have more questions."

"Are we free to go?" Gage touched Nia's elbow as if ready to direct her out of here.

Mario narrowed his eyes at them before nodding. "Yes, you're free to go. But watch yourself."

Watch yourself? Was that a friendly warning?

Or was it a threat?

chapter
thirty-five

GAGE DIDN'T ASK Nia anything about Mario. Not yet.

Instead, he scanned the inside of Avenue 12 one more time. He didn't see anything of note. With his hand still on Nia's elbow, he directed her outside.

It was dark . . . well past midnight. People lingered on the sidewalk. Cried. Comforted each other.

That wasn't to mention the numerous police cars and ambulances parked all along the street.

A couple of news vans had even shown up.

Gage quickly turned away so his and Nia's images wouldn't be caught on camera. As part of his job, he avoided having his image on TV or in the newspaper even. It was too risky.

Right now, it could be risky for Nia also.

He scanned everything around him, needing to make sure they were safe as they walked.

He hadn't seen anyone following them from the

hotel to the club. No one should know they were staying at the Royal Oasis. He'd covered all his bases going to and from the place.

But he still needed to operate on the side of caution.

Once they moved away from the crowds and toward Austin's car, Gage turned to Nia. "You want to talk?"

"Not here."

He couldn't blame her. He'd much rather talk somewhere more private where he could give his full attention to the conversation.

They climbed into Austin's rental car and headed back to the hotel, which wasn't far away.

When they walked into the hotel room, he spotted Austin sitting on the couch. His colleague closed his computer and turned to them.

"I heard what happened at the club," he murmured. "It's on the news. You two okay?"

Gage nodded, instinctively reaching for Nia's back as if to steady her. But maybe the truth was that he found comfort in that touch as well.

"We're fine," Gage told him. "Just shaken up."

"I can imagine." Austin rose. "I won't keep you up too late. I just wanted to make sure you were okay."

"Did you find out anything?" Gage stepped closer.

"I'm still looking, and it's going to take a while. I spent a lot of my time just tracking down information on where the various cameras were located. Then I needed to figure out server information and . . . you know the rest of the drill. Anyway, I'm still working on things, but I was able to obtain one video feed."

"Which one?" Nia stepped closer, joining him on the edge of the living area.

The muscles on Austin's face pulled tighter, almost as if he had bad news. "I was able to get one of you and Rob leaving the restaurant that night."

She sucked in a breath. "And?"

He shook his head, a frown tugging at his lips. "The two of you were alone. And you looked happy and normal as you stepped outside."

"What?" Nia's words sounded breathless.

Austin frowned apologetically again. "I'm sorry. But no one else was with you two, Nia. It was just you and Rob."

Nia felt her head spinning and dropped onto the couch. "How is that even possible?"

Gage slowly lowered himself onto the cushion beside her. "I don't know."

She squeezed the skin between her eyes, beginning to feel a headache pulse there. "So Rob and I left the restaurant alone and happy. Then you saw us walking into Rob's apartment building, and we still looked happy. And we were alone—not under duress. No one else calling the shots." She shook her head. "It doesn't make any sense. No matter which angle I look at it from, I can't make sense of it."

"The situation is confusing."

She glanced behind her and saw Austin disappearing

into one of the bedrooms. He must have sensed she needed some privacy to talk to Gage.

"I'm sorry, Nia," Gage murmured. "But we'll keep trying to find answers. I promise you that."

She glanced up, hoping to convey her gratitude in her gaze. "Thank you. I appreciate that. But part of me is afraid of what I might find out."

"What do you mean?" Gage's eyes narrowed as he studied her face.

"I mean, what if I had some type of mental break? What if I did hurt Rob? And what if I can't remember any of that?"

"If that's true then who's sending you the threats? Who's shooting at you?"

"Someone who needs something from me." She glanced up at him, needing to reach him. "If you notice, these guys have never actually tried to kill me. They've followed me. Fired bullets that missed—maybe on purpose. But they've never tried to kill me. They had more than one chance, including when I was inside Rob's apartment." She shook her head. "Maybe that doesn't make any sense."

Gage squeezed her arm. "No, I know what you're saying."

He could see her dilemma, couldn't he?

He could see where she might be guilty.

She and Gage had just started to bond. Would this change things?

chapter
thirty-six

GAGE DIDN'T WANT to acknowledge that what Nia had said made sense.

But it did.

Those men who had followed them . . . they could have simply wanted to grab her.

Scenarios played out in his head as he tried to make sense of the situation.

If someone had killed Rob and left Nia there . . . why hadn't they killed her? They wanted her alive for a reason. Was that because they wanted someone to blame Rob's death on?

Possibly.

But if that was the case, wouldn't they have sent the photos to the police instead of taunting her with them?

It seemed as if that was the case.

So maybe someone had left Nia alive in order to use those images to manipulate her into getting information on Rob.

Maybe there was more to it than that, even. Maybe this person wanted to manipulate Nia into doing something.

But what would that be? Nia was smart. Really smart. And she had a successful company. She most likely even had a great deal of money.

But those guys didn't seem to be going after any of those things. So what would they want from Nia?

Then there was a third scenario. The one that Nia had just suggested.

The one Gage didn't want to believe.

What if Nia had had some type of mental break, and she *had* done this? Gage didn't see her as that type. But people in high-pressure situations could do things they didn't normally do.

If Nia had killed Rob, why? To keep the app for herself? Because she didn't want to pull out of their deal?

And now maybe these men wanted that information?

No . . . that didn't make sense. There was nothing special about Rob's app. It helped promote relaxation. Gage couldn't see where that had anything to do with this.

Yet Rob had discovered something urgent enough for him to ask Gage to come. What could that have been?

His thoughts continued to swirl.

"You want me to leave?" Nia asked.

Her voice pulled him from his thoughts.

Gage stared at her face. Her dark, rich eyes. The slight

frown on her full lips. The way her curls had seemed to lose some of their luster and bounce.

He swallowed hard before saying, "No, I don't want you to leave."

"I wouldn't blame you if you did."

"We're going to figure this out," he assured her. "We're only just starting."

"I have no recollection of what I was doing twenty-four hours ago. But according to the video footage, I was in Rob's apartment with him. Sometime in there, he died, and we've found no evidence that anyone else was there."

Her words echoed in his mind.

Now more than ever, they needed to figure out what had happened.

And he still had other questions . . . maybe less important questions.

But he still wanted answers.

He turned to her, hoping the subject change might be good for both of them.

Then he asked, "What's your past with Mario?"

Nia swallowed hard at Gage's question.

She knew it was coming. Gage was a perceptive guy. No doubt he'd picked up on the bad vibes between her and Mario.

"We dated," Nia started.

Gage's eyes widened, but he said nothing, just waited for her to continue.

"It didn't end well," she told him. "He wasn't the person I thought he was."

"What do you mean?" Gage asked.

She glanced at her hands, wishing sometimes that she could erase the memories. But they were a part of her. Her relationship with Mario was something she simply needed to learn from. It was the only way to put a positive spin on the situation.

"The two of us met at a benefit for a children's hospital about a year and a half ago," she said. "He was charming and made me laugh. When he asked me out, I didn't hesitate to say yes. Our first few dates went really well. I thought maybe we had a future together."

"I'm assuming something changed."

"I guess you could say *I* changed. I realized I didn't like the way I was living. I didn't like the partying and the jet-setting lifestyle. But Mario did. In fact, sometimes I think that's what he liked more than he actually liked me. He saw me more as an opportunity. I only wish I had seen it sooner."

"I can see why things didn't end well."

Nia shook her head as she remembered. "He came across as someone who was so noble. But the truth was, how he acts is all a façade. He's a master at those things."

"What did he do?"

She rubbed her throat, thoughts racing. "I knew his family had a place down in the Keys. He wanted me to go down there with him, but I couldn't. I had something pressing at work and couldn't get away."

Nia licked her lips, taking a moment to compose herself.

"Then my meeting was canceled," she continued. "I decided to surprise Mario. But when I showed up, he was with someone."

"*With someone* with someone?"

Nia nodded. "Even worse, it turned out the woman was a prostitute. I was horrified. But apparently, Mario had a long history of doing things like that. Many of his cronies knew about it, but they were loyal to him and stayed quiet."

He grunted. "What happened next?"

"I confronted him. He made excuses. But I knew the truth. I left, totally blindsided by all of it. Before I drove off, he begged me not to tell the mayor. Told me no one would believe me anyway. Then he said if I did tell anyone, he'd ruin my reputation."

"Did you tell anyone?"

She licked her lips as that horrible period in her life flooded back into her thoughts. "It's a huge liability having a police chief who sleeps with prostitutes. It's how people become crooked. The wrong person can use those things as leverage to get what they want—including dropped or lessened charges. Besides, if Mario was hiding his involvement with prostitutes, what else was he hiding?"

"Good point," Gage said.

"So I went to the DA." Nia swallowed hard as she

remembered. "He didn't believe me and totally dismissed what I said. Honestly, I think Mario had something on him and that's why he acted the way he did. Mario found out what I'd done, however. That's when he started spreading rumors throughout the department that *I* had cheated on *him*. That I was making up rumors to cover up what I'd done. Most people believed him."

"That's dirty." Disgust rippled through his words.

Nia nodded. "I know. He even sent officers out to harass me. They'd drive past me when I was walking down the street and give me looks. I got parking tickets for no good reason. Got pulled aside for an extra security check at a ballgame. I knew what it meant. It was a warning."

"Did you press the subject anymore?"

"I wanted to. I thought about it. But Mario insisted no one would believe me, and I think he was right. Eventually, I came to accept the fact that one day he'd mess up. I needed to step back and wait for him to get caught in his own lies."

"Probably wise."

Their gazes met.

Gage opened his mouth as if he wanted to say more.

But then he shut it again.

Which was better.

She'd already shared too much. She never talked about the Mario situation anymore. It was too painful. Too frustrating.

But somehow, telling Gage had felt like a relief—especially since he believed her.

She had the crazy desire to reach for him. To fall into his arms.

Or, at least, to dream about what that would be like.

The feelings felt foreign. She had no idea where they came from.

Emotions suddenly seemed to seize her, and she stood. "Well, I should get to sleep. It's been a long day."

Gage stood also and nodded. "Of course. You should get some rest."

But she couldn't ignore the tension stretching between them as they said good night.

chapter
thirty-seven

GAGE AWOKE the next morning feeling restless.

He hadn't been able to sleep much—he'd only gotten a couple of hours of shut-eye at the most. But he was used to surviving on little to no rest. It was part of his training.

Thoughts of his conversation with Nia had kept him up for most of the night.

He tried to put himself in her shoes. To imagine what she'd gone through with Mario.

Every time he thought about it, a surge of anger rushed through him.

Guys like Mario gave men a bad name.

It wasn't even that Gage wanted a relationship with Nia. He'd resigned himself to being single. With the job he did, it was better if he remained unattached. But every once in a while he imagined what it would be like to settle down and have a normal life.

His friend Jonah Gray had done it. He'd left the

Shadow Agency, and now he worked on an idyllic island off the coast of North Carolina. And he was engaged. And he seemed happy.

Was it even possible to have that kind of life while still working for the agency?

Gage had heard rumors that Larchmont didn't want to let people go.

But Jonah had somehow gotten out, so it must be possible.

Gage turned over again, unsure where these thoughts were even coming from.

He loved his job. Loved the adrenaline rush when he tracked down bad guys.

At least he used to.

Right now, he wasn't sure—and being unsure bothered him.

Realizing he wasn't going to sleep, he stood from the couch. The place had only two bedrooms, but Austin had taken one and Nia the other, which was fine.

Gage took a quick shower and threw on some fresh clothes.

By the time he got out, Nia was sitting in a chair reading from the Bible left on a table in the hotel room.

When she looked up at him and smiled, his whole world seemed to stop.

Okay, so maybe he was lying if he said there was nothing between them. That he didn't feel anything. Because he clearly did.

But it was better if he didn't get close to anyone. That motto had kept him alive and thriving for a long time. His life was a small sacrifice to make for the safety of his country.

That mindset had been drilled into him when he went through training for Project Elevate.

His black-ops missions had been intense. Failure would lead to the government denying his affiliation with them.

Then the program had imploded.

He and his teammates had been forced to try to blend in with society—a challenge in itself considering all they'd been through.

Then Larchmont, a former superior in the military, had formed the Shadow Agency and had given them all purpose again.

"Good morning." Nia closed the Bible and curled her legs underneath her, turning to give her full attention to him. "I'm sorry you had to sleep on the couch. If we're here again tonight, I can switch out with you."

He waved her off and sat in the chair next to her. "I was fine. I've slept in much worse places."

She studied his face as if she wanted to ask more questions. "I'm sure you have a lot of stories you could tell from your military days."

"I do. But none that you'd want to hear."

"But what if I did?"

He shrugged. "Maybe I should have said, none that I'm allowed to share."

Her eyebrows rose, but she nodded. "I understand." She paused before asking, "So what's the plan for today?"

He plucked a room service menu from a nearby table.

"First, we order breakfast. I can't start my day without it. Well, I can, but I'm a bear to live with. While we eat, we can talk about what we'll do today. I'll get Austin up if you want to go ahead and order something. Just put it on the tab. My boss owes me one, so I'm going to let him pay for it."

A small smile feathered across her face. "Will do then."

He rose and went to get Austin.

Not because he really needed to wake up his friend.

But because he needed to get away from Nia . . . especially since he realized just how attracted he was to the woman.

Nia took another spoonful of her yogurt and fruit parfait as she prepared a plan for the day.

She'd always been a planner. That quality had helped her to get to where she was. She set goals. Made practical lists on how to reach those goals.

When the original plan didn't work, she'd learned to pivot.

That was what she needed to do now also.

She gave the men a minute to eat their bacon and eggs. When she neared the end of her parfait, she grabbed a small notepad and complementary pen so she could write a few things down.

"Do either of you have any thoughts on how to figure all of this out?" she started.

Maybe she shouldn't take charge of the situation. Maybe she should leave that to Gage since this seemed to be more in his wheelhouse. But she'd always been a go-getter, and this situation wasn't going to change that.

"I think we can rule out Brittany and Darius." Gage picked up his last piece of bacon. "I'm not sure how the shooting last night ties in with all of this. But we can rest assured that Darius isn't going to be able to tell us anything. While I was waiting for breakfast, I called the hospital. He's still in ICU and not allowed visitors."

"Good to know," Nia said. "When we spoke to Brittany last night, I didn't get the impression she knew anything either."

Gage shoved his plate aside before picking up his coffee. "I think we need to look for Cormac. However, that's going to be easier said than done. I'm sure the police have tried to track his cell phone."

"For all we know the police could have found him already," Austin said.

"That's true," Gage conceded. "It hasn't been on the news because I checked. But that doesn't mean anything."

"My gut tells me he hasn't been found," Nia said. "I'm just basing that on the way he disappeared last night. He's a smart man. Rob wouldn't have hired him if he wasn't. And without the resources of the police department, I don't know how we'll find him."

"I agree that it's going to be challenging. We don't want to run all over town without purpose, just hoping that we'll find him."

"Agreed," Nia said, jotting down his name. "I also think we should talk to Hector Backus. Maybe he knows something."

"That's a great idea," Gage said. "I'm going to assume his office probably opens at eight or nine. So as soon as you're ready, I say we go and see if he'll talk. Let's keep the element of surprise by not calling him first."

"That sounds good to me." Nia rose.

Austin ate another piece of his bacon. He'd ordered double meat and was taking his time with his meal. "I'll keep searching the security videos until I find something. But in the meantime, if you need something from me, let me know and I'll be there."

It seemed weird, but Nia was so thankful she was able to team up with these two guys. There was no way she'd be able to find this information by herself, nor would she want to. She might be good with computers and business deals. But guns and tracking down bad guys?

Not at all.

Maybe if they combined all their skills, they could figure out what was going on here.

chapter
thirty-eight

NIA TOOK a shower and dressed in some clothes Gage had purchased in the gift shop downstairs. Then, using her new untraceable phone, she called into the office and told Melissa she'd be late if she came in at all today.

Melissa said that people were starting to talk. That they were wondering what was going on, and Graham seemed especially agitated about her absence.

That didn't surprise Nia because Graham thought he owned the place.

"Remind him that it's my company, and I'm the boss," Nia said. "I'll come in when I can."

There were times when she simply liked doing business but not being the boss and managing people. It was why she'd hired Graham—so he could do that for her as the VP of Operations.

But sometimes he was the one who required the most managing of all.

After her phone call, she found Gage in the living

room. Nia forced herself to ignore the way her heart sped at the sight of him.

"Are you ready?" He checked his phone before sliding it into his pocket.

She nodded and pushed a curl behind her ear. "As ready as I'll ever be."

He nodded toward the door, and they stepped up to it. As per usual, Gage checked the hallway before indicating for her to follow him.

No one else was out and about right now, and that made Nia feel a little better—though she did wonder how long it would be before their hideout was discovered.

Whoever those men chasing her were, they were smart and resourceful. She knew it was probably just a matter of time.

Nia didn't like the thought of that. At least the room was reserved under a different name and on someone else's credit card.

Hector's office was only a couple of blocks away, so it made more sense to walk than it did to drive.

With every step, Nia prayed Hector could provide some answers for them.

Gage watched as Nia talked to the receptionist at the law office.

Nia had a very convincing way about her, which he was certain helped her in the business world. She seemed like a natural when it came to making deals and convincing people to see things her way.

Again, she impressed him, something Gage hadn't been expecting.

No, what he'd been expecting was that she was a murderer.

But he didn't think that. Not anymore.

Even their conversation last night hadn't swayed him otherwise.

He just didn't think Nia had it in her to take someone else's life.

Still, he reminded himself to be cautious and keep his distance. He couldn't let himself get close to people. It would only be a liability.

Several minutes after they arrived, they were ushered into a large, spacious corner office. A thin man with a shock of white hair, a narrow nose with wire-framed glasses, and a stuffy but expensive business suit sat behind the massive desk there.

"Hector . . . good to see you again," Nia started.

The man rose and offered a stiff nod. "You too, Nia. Although I wish it wasn't under these circumstances."

"You and me both." She turned to Gage. "This is Gage, a friend of mine."

Hector offered a nod, a cautious look remaining in his eyes.

They all took seats, and Hector asked, "What brings you this way?"

"I know this is a bit unconventional," Nia started. "But I need to know what happened to Rob."

"Is this about the contract? Because, despite Rob's death, it's already a done deal—although I'm not sure if Rob sent you everything you need for the app. But I'm not sure I'll be able to help you with that."

"No, it's not about that. I'm trying to piece together what happened to Rob between the time we met in my office on Tuesday and the time the two of us had dinner together."

Hector's forehead wrinkled. "So he did have dinner with you?"

Nia's eyebrows rose. "You knew about that?"

"I encouraged him to meet with you. So I'm glad that he did. Although now . . . I suppose it doesn't really mean anything . . ."

"It sounds like you met with him after he was at Nia's office," Gage said. "Is there anything you can tell me about that meeting?"

Hector let out a long breath. "There are things I can't say because of confidentiality. But I *can* tell you that Rob did contact me around three yesterday."

"Do you mind if I ask what he said?" Nia asked.

"He sounded nervous, but he didn't tell me much. Only that something had come up and he'd changed his mind. He wanted to know if the contract was iron-clad."

"And you told him?" Gage asked.

"I told him that it was, unfortunately." Hector nodded slowly. "That The Anderson Group could sue him if he tried to back out and that they'd probably win. He said it might be worth it."

"He asked me at dinner that night if I might change

my mind." Nia frowned. "But he didn't say what had set this in motion."

Hector shrugged. "Unfortunately, he didn't tell me either. But it seemed like a new development. He was gung-ho earlier in the day."

Nia shifted in her seat. "I'm trying to put together a timeline. He left my office around two-thirty on Tuesday. He called me at four asking if we could meet. That's not much time for something to change."

"From what he told me, he went back home to work on his product. That's where he called me from." Hector paused. "His assistant was with him. Maybe you should talk to him."

"Cormac?" Nia murmured, a touch of surprise in her voice.

"Yes, he's the one." Hector nodded in affirmation.

Nia exchanged a look with Gage, and he knew exactly what she was thinking.

Cormac was the missing puzzle piece they were looking for.

They had to figure out a way to find him.

chapter
thirty-nine

GAGE PAUSED ONCE he and Nia were out of the office and downstairs, away from anybody who could hear. "We definitely need to find Cormac."

"I agree," Nia said. "I just don't know how we're going to do that."

Gage had been thinking it through, and there was only one solution in his mind. "I think we need to go to his house."

"You think he's going to be there?" Nia looked up at him with confusion in her gaze.

"Not necessarily. But maybe we'll see something that will indicate where he went. Do you know if he has a roommate?"

Nia shook her head. "I have no idea. I don't really know that much about the man. I only met him once when he came into the office with Rob. And he seemed nice enough. Not like a killer."

Gage nodded and raked a hand through his hair. "I understand. But I still think he could have some answers for us."

"I agree. Let's find his address and get going."

They stepped outside again onto the sunlit street. He glanced around as they did, but he didn't see anybody of interest.

Was it possible that they truly had lost those guys who'd been tracking them? It almost seemed too good to be true.

Regardless, Gage wouldn't let down his guard.

He and Nia hurried along the city blocks until they reached the hotel's parking garage. They used Austin's rental car again. It seemed like a safer bet considering everything that had happened.

Once inside, Gage pulled out his phone and found the address for Cormac. It would take them twenty minutes to get to the Miami suburb. Memories of what had happened yesterday in the parking garage filled his mind.

But so far, everything still seemed to be safe.

Almost too safe.

Gage tried to shake off the thoughts. Instead, he should be thankful they'd lost these guys. But he had no doubt they were still looking for Nia.

He pulled from the garage and followed the directions out of Miami. He kept an eye on everything around him as he did, just to be on the safe side.

"Good job back there," Gage said. "If you didn't

already have a successful career, I might try to recruit you for the agency I work for."

"I'm quite content with what I do," Nia said. "And I don't fully understand everything you guys do."

There was a lot that he wished he could tell her. But he couldn't. He'd signed the confidentiality clause. Besides, the more she knew, the more danger she'd be in.

"Do you see yourself working there for a long time?" she asked.

"That's a good question." He stared out the front window. "Usually, people are in it for life."

Her eyebrows flung up. "Really? It sounds like an exciting life but not necessarily an easy one. Especially if you're doing assignments all over the country. Maybe even the world."

She'd picked up on more of the nuances in what he said than Gage had expected. He would need to be careful.

"Not everyone is meant to settle down." His throat ached as he said the words.

But they needed to be spoken.

They were a good reminder for both of them to keep their distance. That anything between them would never work.

Besides, it wasn't like Gage and Nia really knew each other. In fact, it had been less than two days since they'd first met. So why did it feel like they'd known each other for months?

Gage supposed trauma and stress could do that.

He shoved those thoughts aside as they drove into Cormac's neighborhood.

Maybe this would be the place they finally found some answers.

Nia glanced around as they pulled up to Cormac's house.

The walls were beige concrete, and the house had an orange barrel roof with a brick driveway. Several palm trees surrounded the home. The place was small and not especially fancy but nice, nonetheless.

She expected the police to be stationed outside the place, but she didn't see anyone. She even scanned the cars parked on the street, looking for anyone hunkering down inside who might be a cop in disguise.

But all the vehicles appeared empty.

Curious. Nia would think the police would want to plant someone here in case Cormac came back. Unless they were betting on him not coming back, which could be the case. Or, for all she knew, they could have already found him.

She didn't expect to find the man here. But it seemed as if it would be a disservice to the investigation if she and Gage didn't come here and at least look.

Cautiously, they walked up to the front door, and Gage knocked. He craned his neck, scanning everything around them as he did.

Nia was certain he hadn't let down his guard since all this craziness began, and she could appreciate that.

There was no answer, just as expected.

He knocked again, but there was still no answer.

Again, not a surprise.

"What now?" Nia turned toward him.

Gage scanned the front of the house. Then he walked to a window by the small porch and cupped his hands around his eyes to peer inside. The sun glinted off the glass, making it hard to see.

"Anything?" she asked.

Gage backed up and shook his head. "No, everything looks normal. No signs of a struggle or anything like that."

"Cormac's a smart man. I'm sure he didn't come back. Half of me *did* expect there to be some damage though."

"Me too."

"You're not planning on breaking in, are you?" She stared up at him, curious as to his reaction.

Gage glanced around one more time. "That wouldn't be a good idea. I don't see any cops, but I have a hard time believing they're not keeping their eye on this place."

"My thoughts exactly."

"Let me check out the backyard."

Nia started to follow him around that way when she saw someone step from a neighbor's house. She tensed, wondering if there would be a confrontation.

"Can I help you two?" the neighbor called.

The man was probably in his sixties with a robust

belly, age spots on his face, and nearly nonexistent hair on his head.

Gage paused. "Just looking for Cormac."

"You and the police too. They were here last night and this morning."

"I guess that means you haven't seen him," Nia said.

"Nope. Sure haven't. That's what I told the police too."

Suddenly, a memory hit Nia. A memory of a conversation she'd had with Rob and Cormac.

She looked at the man. "You must be Lillard."

He narrowed his eyes, his shaggy eyebrows becoming one. "Are you a friend?"

She nodded. "I remember Cormac talking about you. He always loved those cookouts you threw for the Fourth of July. And you liked to give him fish after long days out on the charters. The tuna was always his favorite."

His face softened as if her words had caused a temporary trust between them. "He does love his tuna. I told him I would start charging him. Not that I really will."

"We're worried about him and trying to find him," Nia said.

He rubbed his chin. "I figured there was some type of trouble. The police wouldn't tell me anything. Just that they wanted to question him about an investigation."

"We think he might be in trouble," Gage added.

Lillard frowned. "I hate to hear that. I always liked Cormac. He's a fun guy to have around and a good neighbor. Never had to worry about the conversation if he was there."

"Listen, do you have any idea where he may have gone?" Nia said. "If we don't find him before the police do, there's a good chance he'll end up in jail. I don't want to see that happen. I want to help him."

The words felt like the truth, probably because they were. She really *did* like Cormac, and she really didn't think that he would have killed Rob.

Lillard hesitated another moment before saying, "I didn't tell the police this. Something told me not to, and I hope I wasn't wrong. But between you and me, Cormac told me about a fishing cabin his family owns. It actually belongs to his cousin by marriage or something, so it probably couldn't be traced back to him. But he said he liked to go there when he could. He said it was a good fishing spot."

Nia's heart beat harder. "Do you have any idea where this place is?"

"Pretty sure he said it was on the Miami River, out near the Glades. Near an old fishing camp maybe. Can't remember the exact name."

Nia knew the basic area. But based on the size of the Glades, going door to door to find him was an impossibility.

"I wish I could give you a specific address," Lillard continued. "But he did show me a picture of the place once. It's an old shanty-style cabin. Painted a light-blue color and surrounded by trees. I hope that helps."

Nia glanced at Gage, and they exchanged a nod.

"This was a huge help," Nia said. "Thank you so much."

"If you find him . . . don't let anybody hurt him." Lillard's voice cracked. "He may be the life of the party, but he doesn't have that much common sense. I think he needs somebody watching out for him."

chapter
forty

"GOOD WORK BACK THERE," Gage told Nia as they headed down the road. "I'm assuming you didn't just make all that up."

Nia shook her head. "No, a memory came back to me. The neighbor is right. Cormac is a talker—very engaging and a natural storyteller. I didn't know if he would ever get out of my office that day he came with Rob. He seemed too content to entertain anybody he was talking to."

"I suppose his talkativeness worked in our favor."

"It sounds like it did." She leaned back in her seat. "Do you think the police know about this cabin?"

"If it's in the name of a non-family member then there's a good chance they don't. And it would be the perfect place for him to go. Escaping to a hotel would be difficult because Cormac would probably have to use a credit card. The police, no doubt, are tracing those."

"Do you think he's guilty?" Nia asked. "Are we trying to track down a killer?"

"I can't tell you that." Gage stared out the windshield. "But we *will* need to be careful. That's certain."

"So this is what we know so far." Nia leaned back and sighed. "Rob came to my office at two. He seemed happy. He left at two-thirty, and he got a text as he left then a phone call from that same number. Around three, he called Hector."

"He would have barely had time to get back to his apartment." Gage readjusted his hands on the steering wheel and stole a glance at her.

"That's true. And Cormac would most likely meet him at his place, I'm assuming. Rob wouldn't have even had time to pick him up. Maybe Cormac was waiting for Rob when he got back from our meeting."

"That's right," Gage agreed. "And in that short amount of time, something changed. Rob decided he wanted out. At four, he called to set up dinner with you. Then around four-thirty he called me to ask if I would come."

Nia turned toward him. "The fact he called you is interesting because I've been assuming this was a contract or financial matter. But I don't know why he would call you if that was the case."

Gage had had those exact same thoughts. "Rob wouldn't have called me for those reasons. I wouldn't have been that much help to him. The only reason he would have called me . . ."

"Would be if he was in danger," Nia finished.

Gage gripped the wheel harder and nodded. "Exactly. So within that hour, he went from being happy to feeling like his life was in danger. It just doesn't make sense."

"You're right, it doesn't." Nia shook her head and stared out the window. "Hopefully, Cormac will be able to offer us some answers . . . if we're able to find him."

Nia stared at the cabin where Cormac might possibly be staying.

It looked just like Lillard had described it with the light-blue siding. They'd searched along the river near the old fish camp until they'd found something that matched.

The place was set far off the gravel road, and grass and reeds grew up around it. Several live oak trees, each with moss hanging from their branches, stood around the place. A glimmering lake sparkled in the background.

This was an older area, mostly used by sportsmen. The glamour of Miami was absent in favor of an old Florida feel.

The place was also far enough inland that Nia and Gage would need to watch out for alligators.

She swallowed hard at that thought.

Her gaze drifted to a small garage beside the bungalow. Nia would bet Cormac's car was inside.

Gage turned toward her. "I'd tell you to stay in the car while I check things out, but I have a feeling you don't want to do that."

"I'd rather go with you than sit here." There was no need to skirt around the truth. "But I don't want to hinder you from doing your job."

He stared at her another moment before nodding. "If you stay behind me and promise not to do anything rash then you can come out with me. Is it a deal?"

"Deal. And if it makes you feel better, I'm not usually impulsive . . . not unless I wake up beside a dead body." Grief flashed through Gage's eyes, and regret instantly filled Nia. "I'm sorry. I know he was your friend, and I didn't mean—"

Gage held up a hand to stop her. "You don't have to apologize. I understand what you're saying. Sometimes it still hasn't sunk in that Rob is dead."

"It takes time for these things. I'm sorry you have to go through that."

He drew in a deep breath and then nodded to the house. "Let's go see if Cormac is inside."

Nia nodded, thankful Gage had been gracious. Then she followed him out of the car, carefully closing her car door as to not alert Cormac they were there.

She remained behind Gage just as she promised as they walked toward the house. Gage paused by the garage and peered inside.

"That's his car. I had Austin look it up, and he texted me the information earlier. Cormac is here."

Gage reached for the gun at his waist but held it just out of sight.

Then he knocked at the door. "Cormac. I'm Gage, a friend of Rob's. Nia is here also. We need to talk. We know you didn't kill anybody. And we need answers about Rob."

Nia waited, hoping to hear footsteps, some sign of life.

There was nothing.

After a few more minutes, Gage peered through the window atop the door.

"What do you see?" Nia asked.

"Someone's been here recently. A coffee cup is on the table, and a set of keys are on the table. But I don't see any signs of life."

Temporary relief washed through her. At least Gage hadn't seen a dead body.

Nia hadn't even realized it, but another death had been her biggest fear coming here.

One was already too many.

"Let's walk around the house and see what else we can find," Gage said.

She followed him, and they peered in each window. However, they saw nothing of help.

When they reached the back side of the house, Nia pointed to a small pier jutting into the river. "Gage . . . it looks like there was a boat here."

"How can you tell?"

"Look at the way the ropes are thrown over the pilings—and they're still wet. I bet a boat was docked here, and someone took it out . . . recently."

They walked closer to the water and spotted several boats on the river. Nia halfway feared Gage would suggest stealing one, just like he'd "borrowed" that car yesterday. But they had no way of reaching any of them without having a boat themselves.

"Maybe Cormac likes to go fishing when he's stressed," Nia said. "Maybe he's out there somewhere."

Gage nodded as he stared with a locked jaw at the sparkling river. "You're probably right."

Nia glanced up at him. "Do we wait for Cormac to come back?"

"Who knows how long that's going to take." Gage frowned. "I say we come back later. In the meantime, we have more investigating to do."

Before they could step back, the reeds rustled.

At just that moment, an alligator scurried from the water, stopping mere feet in front of them.

Nia froze as she stared at the beast, wondering what it would do next.

chapter
forty-one

GAGE WATCHED the gator and put his arm out, blocking Nia from getting any closer. He had his gun, but he didn't want to shoot the creature—not unless he absolutely had no other choice.

"Slowly back away," he murmured. "No sudden moves. We should be fine."

The gator continued to eye them.

Gage wasn't an alligator expert, but he knew they were fast runners. They couldn't sustain the speed for long—but in this case, it would be long enough.

The beast let out a low sound, almost like a growl.

Then it took another lurching step toward them.

Nia gasped beside him.

"On the count of three, run," Gage murmured. "One, two, three!"

They darted away from the creature.

Gage looked back. Saw it was following.

It kept following them across the yard.

They reached the garage, and Gage saw some cement blocks stacked there. "This way!"

He scrambled up them, pulling Nia behind him.

The gator paused, started to climb up after them.

It made the hissing sound again.

"Gage . . ." Nia's voice shook.

"Just wait."

He hoped his bet paid off.

A moment later, the gator lost interest. He lowered himself back onto all fours and strutted away, almost as if it had only wanted to run them off.

Gage's shoulders relaxed.

That was the last thing he'd expected.

He jumped down and offered a hand to help Nia.

She landed beside him, and they hurried back to the car.

Once they were safely inside, she said, "I think we should go back to my office."

Gage cast her a side glance as he pulled away from the fishing cabin. "What is that going to prove?"

"Prove? Nothing. But I have the contract there as well as a copy of the patent for the app."

"That's risky going back there," Gage reminded her. "Those guys are probably watching your office building."

"I know. But I wonder if there could be some answers there. We could be careful."

Gage knew there were some precautions they could take. But it was still risky.

"If you think that's a good idea then I'm game," he

finally said. "Maybe there will be something in there that we missed."

As they headed back down the road, his thoughts continued to race.

On a whim, he pulled into a department store.

Nia looked up at him in confusion. "Shopping therapy?"

"Not quite." He let out an airy chuckle. "You're going to need some new clothes. Plus, the more we can conceal our appearance the better. Maybe pick up a hat. Sunglasses. Something that's going to make us less obvious."

"Seems smart."

"Your hair is pretty unique as well. Maybe pull it back into a bun. It could buy us some time because I'm sure if these guys are still looking for you then they'll be looking for your long, curly hair."

"Got it."

"I have some cash we can use to pay, just in case." Gage cut the engine. "But let's not take too much time."

"I've never been a big shopper, so I'll be quick."

Gage pulled the keys from the ignition and grabbed the door handle. "Perfect. Then let's go."

A half hour later, Nia and Gage had finished shopping and had grabbed some lunch from a fast-food restaurant along the route.

Nia's hair was pulled back into a tight bun. She wore

a black ball cap that formed nicely to her head along with sunglasses.

She'd ditched the designer clothes—and by ditched she meant put them in a bag in the back of the car. They were too expensive to throw away. Instead, she wore some jeans with a plain blue top and some tennis shoes.

Gage had also bought another ball cap and a black T-shirt.

She hoped Gage was right, and the change of clothes would buy them some time.

But as soon as they exited the elevator on her floor, her employees gave her strange looks. This was not Nia's normal attire. They probably thought something was wrong.

Add Gage walking beside her, and people began whispering to each other.

The first person to approach her was Graham. He rushed from his office and fell into step beside her as she headed to her office.

"I've been trying to call you, and you're not answering your phone," he complained.

"I've been busy. Sorry."

"I would think taking my call would be high on your priority list considering I'm in charge of operations and this is your company." His voice sounded terse and almost accusatory.

"I appreciate your opinion, Graham, and I'll get right on that." Nia didn't want to sound snippy, but she didn't like Graham talking down to her. As founder and CEO, she expected a certain level of respect.

"What have you been up to?" He remained in step beside her. "With Rob's death, we have to figure out how we'll handle this as a company."

She paused, Gage beside her. "I'm well aware that we need to handle that. I've been working on some things."

Graham stared at her. "Are you sure about that? Because I don't feel like you realize the gravity of this situation. We have obligations. We've already signed the deal with Apple, Google, Amazon, even Blackberry."

"Like I just told you, I'm aware and I'm on it. When I have an update to give you, I will. Now, if you'll excuse me." She continued past him.

Graham started to say something more, but Gage cleared his throat, and the man suddenly retreated a step.

Before Graham could badger her anymore, Nia continued toward her office. She nodded at Melissa. Her assistant must have taken one look at Nia's face and known better than to ask any questions. Nia was most definitely not in the mood to talk right now.

Instead, she led Gage into her office. As soon as they were inside, Nia shut the door and let out a breath.

"He's a real peach." Gage crossed his arms as he positioned himself near the door.

"Isn't he, though? He's in charge of operations around here, but sometimes he gives himself a little more power than he should. Unless I stand my ground, people will walk all over me. Being a woman in business has its challenges."

"I'm sure that's true. But I think that you handled yourself well back there."

She offered a grateful smile. "Thank you. I caught that little exchange you had with Graham. I appreciate that too. Saved me some time having to argue with him."

Then she turned and looked at the wall of filing cabinets in her office.

"This is where I keep paper copies," she told him. "I know it's old school, and most people want to store information on their computer. I usually keep digital copies as well, but I always worry they could be altered in some way. Our best bet will be to look at the hard copies."

She began to rifle through the files, trying to find what she needed. Then she paused and let out a heavy breath before continuing to search the filing cabinet again.

"What's wrong?" Gage stepped closer.

She shook her head and paused, resting her hands on top of the rows of manilla folders. "They're not here."

"What do you mean they're not here?"

"I mean, this is where the files on Rob and his app should be." She looked up at Gage and shook her head, not bothering to hide the frustration in her gaze. "They're gone."

Gage cocked his head in thought. "Maybe they got filed in the wrong place."

Nia twisted her lips into a half frown and cocked her head to the side. "It's a possibility. But I put them here myself so it's highly unlikely."

"You said there were electronic versions of the files too, right? So we could just check them."

"That's right." She rushed to her desk and unlocked her computer using a special facial scanner her company had helped broker a deal to sell to high-security companies.

Then she searched through her files.

Several minutes later, she leaned back in her chair and ran a hand over her face.

"I take it it's not good news," Gage muttered as he paced away from the window, where he was keeping watch, and walked toward her.

"My files are gone." Nia ran a hand over her face again as tension stretched through each of her muscles. "Both versions of them. Someone's been in my office. Took my files and got on my computer. Wiped those out too. I need to figure out who."

chapter
forty-two

GAGE WASN'T certain he'd heard Nia correctly. "They're gone? You don't have backup copies of your files on a Cloud somewhere?"

"I checked the backup. These files are gone from that also." Her jaw hardened. "I've got to pull up my security cameras. See who has been in here. First, let me talk to Melissa."

She stuck her head out the door and called her assistant into the office. Gage listened carefully, curious to hear what would transpire.

Melissa—who couldn't be any more than twenty-three, twenty-four years old—rushed to her feet, knocking a stack of papers from her desk in the process. "What's going on?"

"Has anyone been in my office the past two days?" Nia asked, helping her assistant to gather papers.

"Besides you?" Melissa grabbed the last of the papers, took the stack from Nia, and then straightened.

"That's right," Nia said. "Has anyone come in here while I was gone?"

Melissa swung her head back and forth, her motions still jerky with anxiety. "No, I haven't seen anybody. As far as I know it's been locked."

"So you didn't let anybody in for any reason?" Nia locked her gaze with Melissa's. "Even a janitor or somebody in tech looking at the computer?"

"No, no one." Melissa wrung her hands together. "Is everything okay?"

"I'm missing some files that were here on Tuesday."

Melissa's eyes widened. "I haven't seen anything. I've been getting into the office every day at nine o'clock, and yesterday I didn't leave until five."

"Was anybody in the office before you got here?"

Her eyes wavered back and forth with thought. "Nancy in accounting. You know she always likes to get here early. And maybe Jeff in marketing. But I didn't see either of them coming this way. Like I said, your door was locked."

"Where do you keep the spare key?" Gage leaned against the desk with his arms crossed.

"It's in the safe behind my desk," Melissa said. "Near the island."

"Who has the combination to the safe?" Gage continued.

"Just me and Ms. Anderson. That's it." Melissa offered an affirmative nod.

Nia and Gage exchanged another look.

Something wasn't adding up here.

Nia thanked Melissa and dismissed her.

Then Nia went to her computer. "I'm going to look at this security footage myself."

Then she began tapping away at the keyboard.

Gage's lungs tightened as he waited to see what they might find.

Nia felt Gage standing behind her, watching what was on her screen.

She was fine with that. There was nothing there that he shouldn't see.

She started with the night that Rob had been murdered. There was a wide-angle camera right outside her office. However, most people didn't know it was there because it was hidden behind a plant. One of the companies she worked with had developed the small cameras, and she'd decided to keep one for herself.

She started by watching herself leave the office at six. She closed the door behind her and double-checked the lock, just like she always did. Melissa was gone already because Nia had worked a little later than usual.

For the longest time, no one was on the screen. Then at seven-thirty, Jeff wandered to Melissa's desk. He poked around as if looking for something.

"Who is that?" Gage narrowed his eyes.

"Jeff. He's the VP of Finance and a pretty low-key guy."

Nia held her breath, waiting to see what else he did.

Would he reach for the safe?

He didn't. A few minutes after nosing around, he walked away and didn't come back on screen.

She fast-forwarded through the rest of that night.

Nothing else was in the footage.

She continued to fast-forward through the next day.

She saw Melissa come in. Later, Nia came into the office. Graham went into her office and left the door open to speak with her for a few minutes.

Then Graham left, just as Nia remembered. She closed her door before leaving a few minutes later.

Melissa left at five p.m., just as she said.

Nia frowned, but she wasn't ready to give up yet.

If those files went missing, it had to be between the time she left last night and this morning when Melissa came in.

The answers should be in here *somewhere*.

She fast-forwarded.

"What about that Jeff guy?" Gage lingered behind her, and she was all too aware of his presence there. "What do you think he was doing?"

"I'm not sure." She swallowed the lump in her throat and tried to cast off the thoughts of how close Gage was. "But Jeff didn't appear to take anything. For all I know, he was looking for a paper clip."

Despite that, she kept Jeff's image at the back of her mind.

At one-thirty a.m., Nia slowed the video feed, unsure if she was seeing correctly.

"You see that too?" she murmured.

"I do." Gage's voice stiffened.

A figure wearing all black, including a mask, paused outside her office door.

Nia watched to see what would happen next.

chapter forty-three

GAGE LEANED CLOSER to the screen, anxious to see what was happening.

The man in black turned his back to the camera. The next instant, he picked the lock and opened the door to Nia's office. Stepped inside. Left the door open.

The shadow moved toward the filing cabinets. That was all they could see because of the angle and the darkness. Whatever he did inside Nia's office remained a mystery.

Less than five minutes later, the man emerged again. He tucked the files into his coat.

Then he seemed to look right at the camera, almost as if he knew it was there.

A corner of his mouth lifted in a smirk.

Strange.

Nia paused the video as the man stared at the camera.

"I can't believe this." She shook her head. "He looks so . . . smug."

"He knew he was being recorded and didn't care."

"And he's wearing so much clothing it's impossible to tell anything about him. But he knew the files were there." She leaned back and pressed her eyes closed a moment as if trying to sort her thoughts.

"Do you think it was Jeff?"

Her eyes opened again, and she shrugged. "I don't know. I don't know why Jeff would be involved with this. He doesn't seem like the type. I suppose that most people, if they were looking for a file, would assume they were in my office in these filing cabinets. It doesn't necessarily mean it was one of my employees."

"I didn't say it was." Gage made sure to keep his words tempered and even, not wanting to stir up any more emotions than necessary. "I'm just trying to figure things out."

Nia rose, walked to the door, and leaned out toward Melissa. "Any idea why Jeff would have been poking around at your desk yesterday?"

Gage watched through the open door and saw Melissa's expression.

The woman's eyes widened, and she quickly—almost too quickly—shook her head. "I have no idea. Why?"

"Just curious. But you don't normally talk to him, do you? He wouldn't have been getting anything for you?"

Melissa shook her head again. "I didn't ask him to. Did he take something off my desk?"

"I'm just asking questions. I need you to call him and ask him to meet me in my office."

"Of course." She lifted her phone and dialed. A

moment later she frowned. Pushed a button on the phone. "There was no answer. Let me try his assistant instead."

This time when she dialed, someone did answer.

When Melissa ended the call, she looked back up at Gage and Nia. "Jeff called in sick today. I guess if you want to talk to him, you'll have to either call him or pay him a visit."

Called in sick? Gage mused. What were the odds that that wasn't a coincidence?

Nia paced her office, considering all her options. "What should I do? Should I tell the police?"

"I wouldn't." Gage lingered near the window. "Not yet. Not until you know something more."

"Jeff seems nice. I can't see why he would do something like this."

"The person who broke in picked the lock. He knew what he was doing."

Nia shook her head. "This just isn't making any sense."

Gage sighed before walking to the window and peering out. Nia knew exactly what he was doing.

He was still on guard. Still looking for trouble. Still ready to protect her.

Her throat tightened with emotion at the thought.

He was nearly a stranger, yet he'd already done so much for her.

His acts hadn't gone unnoticed.

She observed his strong profile a moment before asking, "Do you see anything?"

"Nothing notable. But everything has been awfully quiet today, don't you think?"

She'd had the same thought but didn't want to voice it aloud. "Yes, it has been."

Maybe these guys had what they wanted.

Or maybe this was the calm before the storm.

Her phone buzzed, and she glanced at the screen.

An unknown number.

Her heart beat faster. She had no idea what she would see on the other side of this.

Once she clicked it, it opened an image on her screen.

She gasped. "It's my sister . . ."

The words below it read: **Do what we say or your sister will die.**

No . . .

As Nia looked at the image closer, she noticed her sister's wrists were bound to the arms of a wooden chair. That her eyes were red as if she'd been crying.

Someone had abducted Sophia.

And it was all Nia's fault.

If only she'd complied with their demands, this would have never happened.

chapter
forty-four

GAGE PLACED a hand on Nia's shoulder, compassion flooding him. "I'm sorry."

As tears began rolling down her face, he prodded her up from the seat and wrapped his arms around her. Nia leaned into the hug.

Gage would hold her as long as she needed to be held.

This had to be a shock to her. It would be for anyone.

More than anything he wanted to comfort her.

"I just can't believe this," she muttered into his chest. "Why would these men go after my sister?"

"These guys are going to do anything to get what they want." He gently stroked her back.

Nia sniffled again before stepping back. She grabbed a tissue from her desk, running it under her eyes and then wiping her nose. "They want to make this personal."

"They want to hit you where it hurts."

"What can they possibly want from me? It appears

they already have all the files and even the contract. They killed Rob—the one person they could have gotten more information from. Why target me?"

"I don't know what they're up to, Nia." Gage's voice remained gentle. "But there's one person I know who might have some of those answers."

She looked up at him. "Cormac?"

"Yes. Cormac. We need to go back to the cabin and see if he's back from that boating trip yet. We don't have any time to waste." A new sense of urgency pressed on Gage.

As soon as they climbed into the car, Gage's phone rang.

Nia's heart pounded harder as she anticipated more bad news.

She couldn't get her sister's image out of her head. Poor, poor Sophia. She didn't deserve any of this.

She'd already gone through so much with her illness. Why did these men have to drag her into this?

The thought was enough to make Nia cry. But it also strengthened her resolve.

She'd do anything to get her sister back. *Anything*. And that was exactly what these people were anticipating.

What would these men demand of her?

Gage answered the phone, and Austin's face came across the screen. "Hey. I've been searching other video feeds, and I found something that may interest you. I'm going to send you a clip of it, okay?"

"Sounds great."

They ended the call, and he told Nia while they waited.

Nia nearly felt sick to her stomach as the seconds ticked by. What would be on the video? What if it was proof Nia did have something to do with this?

She could hardly handle the thought.

The seconds crawled by with agonizing slowness.

Finally, Gage's phone beeped, and he hit the link Austin had sent.

Nia leaned closer and caught the whiff of Gage's piney cologne. She'd noticed it earlier when they'd hugged, but she hadn't been in the mental state to enjoy it.

Right now, the aroma brought her a temporary burst of comfort.

She shoved that thought aside as a video began playing on the screen.

It was of Rob's apartment building.

The footage was from a camera near the front door that picked up everyone coming and going. The time stamp at the bottom read three a.m.

"I woke up about three-thirty," Nia murmured.

Her lungs felt frozen as she continued to wait.

Then she saw it.

A man walked into the building.

She squinted, needing to be certain her eyes were not deceiving her.

But they weren't.

That man was Cormac.

He'd gone into Rob's apartment building on the night Rob was murdered.

It was looking more and more like he might be their guy.

chapter forty-five

GAGE'S THOUGHTS raced as he headed down the road.

He could hardly believe his eyes.

But that had *definitely* been Cormac going into Rob's apartment building. Had he done that so he could kill Rob and frame Nia?

Maybe this guy was guilty.

Because apparently Austin hadn't seen anyone else suspicious enter or leave the building.

He reminded himself that someone could have altered the video. After all, he'd done it. And someone had removed the footage of Nia coming into the apartment building.

But if that wasn't the case . . . did that just leave Cormac?

Gage didn't know, but he didn't like this. However, he and Nia were slowly inching closer to answers.

They would need to be careful. These guys had Nia's

sister . . . a twist he'd not seen coming.

They pulled up to the fishing cabin again. This time, Gage parked farther down the road.

He wanted to keep the element of surprise.

Nia's phone buzzed again. "It's from the same people who sent me the photo of Sophia."

"What does it say?"

She stared at the screen. "That I need to bring them the cyber key by eleven a.m. tomorrow or she'll die." Her voice cracked.

"The cyber key?" Gage asked.

Realization rolled over her features. "It's something Rob developed. How could I have forgotten? It's this extra layer of security for his apps. No one can access them without it."

"You have that information?"

She shook her head. "No, only Rob had it."

"So why would they think you had it?"

She thought about it a moment before shrugging. "I have no idea. Except that they're desperate. Maybe they think I can find it or figure it out."

"Can you?"

"No, not really. That's the purpose of the key." She sighed. "I . . . I don't know what to do."

"Ask where to meet." Gage nodded toward her phone.

With trembling fingers, she typed the words.

The sender responded with, "We'll let you know closer to the time."

Nia swallowed hard. "I only have eighteen hours,

Gage."

His throat tightened. "We'll figure something out. Starting with Cormac." He nodded at the man's house. "Maybe he can help."

This time, Nia wouldn't walk up to the house with him. Not after seeing that video of Cormac.

From Gage's position on the side of the road, he could see the backyard. "The boat is back."

Nia glanced at the vessel bobbing in the water. "Yes, it is."

That should mean that Cormac was back also.

Now it was time to find some answers.

Nia understood why Gage wanted her to stay put. But that didn't mean she liked it.

As she watched Gage approach the house, she gripped the armrest.

She also kept an eye out for that alligator. So far, she hadn't seen it.

It was getting dark outside now, which could work to their advantage or disadvantage, depending.

She wanted to be out there. Wanted to help him.

If they could talk to Cormac . . .

He could tell them what was going on.

Then maybe Nia could help her sister.

Or what if he was the one who took Sophia?

Her throat tightened.

But that theory didn't feel right. Cormac was on the

run. Hiding out. Not in a position to grab Sophia.

Nia's thoughts raced as she tried to make sense of everything.

She watched as Gage went to the front door. He didn't knock. Instead, he crouched low and lifted his head to look in the window.

The shades at the front of the house appeared to be drawn. She thought there might be a light on inside, but she couldn't be certain.

Gage began to walk around back.

She held her breath. Soon, he'd be out of sight and Nia wouldn't know what was going on.

She didn't like that thought.

But Gage seemed perfectly capable of taking care of himself. She had to remind herself of that fact.

She continued to watch.

Then Gage was gone. Out of sight. Behind the house.

She pressed her eyelids together and prayed he would be okay. That he'd stay safe.

Still, she could hardly breathe.

She waited.

And waited.

Then a sound split the air.

Gunfire.

Nia's heart rate ratcheted.

Had Gage pulled the trigger?

Or had it been Cormac?

Without thinking, she opened the car door and darted toward the back of the house.

chapter
forty-six

GAGE FELT the bullet whiz by his ear and jumped out of the way.

Thankfully, the red-headed man holding the gun in the doorway was a bad shot.

But even bad shots got lucky sometimes.

Cormac raised his gun again, ready to fire. A wild look captured his gaze.

"Wait!" Gage shouted. "I'm not here to hurt you."

The handgun trembled in Cormac's hands, and sweat poured down his face as he stared at Gage. His jerky motions made it clear he could change his mind at any time and pull the trigger.

"How did you find me?" Cormac demanded.

"It's not important. I just want to talk."

Cormac extended the gun farther, the weapon still trembling uncontrollably in his hands. "I know who you are. You want to kill me. Just like you killed Rob."

Gage raised his free hand, not daring to take his other

hand off his gun. "I'm telling you, I'm not here to hurt you. I want answers."

Cormac stared at him, clearly uncertain.

How would Gage convince him to talk?

The guy was on edge.

If he pulled that trigger again . . .

"Cormac, we just want to talk," a gentle voice said behind them.

Nia. Gage's jaw hardened. She hadn't stayed in the car like he'd asked.

Now she might get hurt too . . .

Cormac's gaze drifted to her, and his features seemed to soften. "Nia?"

"We've been trying to find you." She moved closer, her hands in the air to prove she wasn't a threat. "Someone's trying to kill me. They're coming after you too, aren't they?"

Cormac lowered his gun slightly. "Did anyone follow you here?"

"They didn't," Gage said. "I checked the entire drive."

"I didn't do anything." Cormac shook his head with such small motions that his skin almost seemed to vibrate. "I'm afraid nobody's going to believe me. I know the police are looking for me. I saw it on the news. My face is plastered everywhere, but it wasn't me. I didn't kill Rob or shoot that guy in the club. I promise!"

"Can we come in?" Nia nodded to the door. "You can tell us your story. Maybe we can help."

Gage stared at Cormac, curious how the man would react.

After a moment of thought, Cormac lowered his gun. "I guess it would be all right. Come in."

Gage and Nia rushed through the door and into the house before the man could change his mind.

Nia sat on the edge of the couch, anxious to hear what Cormac had to say. Based on his jerky motions, tempestuous gaze, and shallow breathing, he was frightened. Really frightened.

"The police think I shot that man at the club." Cormac paced, but at least he'd put his gun down.

But Nia knew Gage still didn't trust him. Probably rightfully so. She wasn't 100 percent sure she trusted Cormac either.

"You were at the club that night." Gage leveled his gaze with Cormac. "We saw you."

"I got a text saying I should go there and meet someone. I've been getting these texts, and the sender is threatening to go to the police and tell them I killed Rob." Sweat beaded on Cormac's forehead.

Nia's heart beat harder. "What?"

"I even got a text the night Rob died, saying I needed to go to his apartment. I knocked, but he didn't answer. I used the code he'd given me to open the door. But when I walked in . . ." His voice cracked, and he rubbed his throat. Then he dragged his gaze up to meet Nia's. "I saw you."

"I didn't do anything," she assured him. "I promise you I didn't."

"I didn't think you would. Besides, I knew you couldn't text me. You were unconscious on the floor. I knew something was up. So as soon as I saw the scene, I ran. I didn't know what else to do."

"So you went to Avenue 12 last night, but you didn't find the person who told you to meet them there, correct?" Gage directed the conversation back to the original purpose.

"That's right. Then I started to leave, but I heard the gunfire. I ran, just like everyone else. I was afraid I'd get shot. Then I heard the police thought I was guilty. I knew I couldn't stick around town."

Nia leaned forward, her elbows resting on her legs. "Whoever is threatening you is also threatening me. I think both of us are being set up and used as pawns."

Cormac froze from his pacing. "What? Really?"

She nodded. "We have to figure out who's behind this, and I'm hoping that you might have some answers for us."

"That's all I have been thinking about. How I want answers."

"Have you thought of anything?" Gage asked.

He ran a hand over his face. "No, entire sections of my memory seem to be wiped . . . It's hard to explain."

The blood drained from Nia's face, and her pulse quickened. "I know exactly what you're talking about."

chapter
forty-seven

GAGE LISTENED to the conversation with interest.

Whatever had happened to Nia had happened to Cormac as well . . .

He hoped that with more questions and digging they'd be able to find some type of commonality to give them answers. Something very strange was going on here.

"We're trying to put together the timeline of what happened to Rob before he died," Gage told Cormac. "We understand you were there with Rob when he had a change of heart about this deal he'd made with The Anderson Group. Could you tell us about that?"

Cormac shook his head then ran a hand through his red hair, leaving the coarse strands standing on end. "I wish I could. I knew Rob had a meeting with The Anderson Group. He asked me to meet him afterward at his place because he wanted to work out a few kinks in the program. I was waiting for him when he got back to his apartment after his meeting with you. He seemed upset but didn't explain why. We fiddled with the program for a few minutes. After that, everything is blank."

"For how long?" Nia stared at Cormac from her position on the couch.

"I don't remember anything else until about eleven o'clock that night," Cormac continued. "I was sitting on the couch in my house trying to figure out what had just happened. I was so confused. How had I lost hours of my time? Later I got the text saying I needed to go to Rob's. I tried to call him first, but he didn't answer. I thought it was weird. Then I got there and . . ."

He didn't have to finish.

Nia leaned closer. "Cormac, I'm missing big chunks of time too, and I'm trying to figure out why. Do you have any ideas?"

Nia watched as Cormac tugged at his collar, sweat still pouring from him.

"Earlier in the week, Rob said he thought he'd discovered something new," Cormac started. "He didn't tell me what."

"Was it some kind of tech?" Nia felt desperate for more information—even if it might seem insignificant to Cormac.

"He honestly didn't say. But I know he was playing with some other ideas. He was brilliant and creative, and he always liked to explore these different ideas. Besides,

I'm not sure how tech would have caused a memory lapse. I wondered if it was something else entirely."

"Like maybe a serum?" Nia asked. "Something that could have been put in our drinks?"

Cormac's face went paler. "I *do* remember having a drink while I was there. It didn't taste strange or anything."

"If we wanted to find out more on whatever Rob was working on, how could we do that?" Gage asked.

"I'm glad you brought that up," Cormac said. "Because when Rob bought that apartment, one of the reasons he picked it wasn't just the view. It has a safe room."

"A safe room?" Nia hadn't been expecting to hear that.

"Yeah, you know like the ones people have in case someone breaks into their house and they need to hide."

"I mean, I know what a safe room is." Nia made sure to keep her voice gentle and not snappy. "But what does that have to do with all of this?"

"As soon as Rob saw the place, he knew *exactly* what he wanted to use it for. He wanted to set up a space to keep his ideas safe."

"Kind of like the cyber key he developed?" Nia licked her lips after asking the question, knowing she could be treading on dangerous ground.

Cormac nodded.

"You don't know where he kept information on this key, do you?" Gage asked.

"No, he was private about it. But I'm sure he wrote it

down somewhere, just in case. I told him he should patent it. Really, the technology he developed for it was brilliant."

"You said he had some type of workshop or office in that safe room?" Nia clarified.

Cormac nodded. "Exactly. No one knows about it. He even had the realtor erase any mentions of it from the archived listings."

Nia and Gage exchanged a look.

"Where is it in the apartment?" Gage asked.

"You have to go through the closet in his master bedroom," Cormac said. "If you move some boxes, you'll find a door there. But you need a code to get in."

"Do you know what that code is?" Nia asked.

Cormac nodded. "As a matter of fact, I do."

Nia sucked in a breath.

Maybe this was just the lead they'd been searching for.

chapter
forty-eight

NIA TURNED to Gage as soon as they climbed back into the car. "What do you think?"

"I believe the man. I think he's scared and confused."

She rubbed her arms, chilled after the conversation. "What happened to Cormac sounds an awful lot like what happened to me."

"I agree. And it's unnerving. We have to figure out what's happening to cause this memory loss."

"We need to go back to Rob's place and see if we can get into that safe room. Maybe there are answers there. Maybe we could even find the cyber key."

"I agree. That was my thought also." His gaze narrowed as he turned toward her. "But I'm not sure it's a good idea if you go, Nia."

"Why wouldn't I go?" She studied his expression. The creases at his eyes. The way his lips pressed together. The tautness of his jaw.

"It's not that I don't think you should be there." His voice softened. "I just don't want you to get hurt."

His words sounded almost tender, and the emotion did something strange to her heart. It almost sounded as if Gage cared.

The two of them hadn't known each other long. Was it even possible that their feelings for each other had grown that rapidly?

Nia wasn't looking for romance. But something about Gage was different. He didn't discount her like so many people had in her life, nor did he seem to care about her money.

She swallowed back the feelings, knowing this wasn't the time to focus on her relationship with Gage.

"It's already dark outside," she started. "I think we should go to Rob's place now and see what we can find out. I'm willing to take the risk. Besides, I know the tech world. I may be able to help you, depending on what we find inside."

Gage stared at her another moment before finally nodding. "Okay then. I won't try to talk you out of it. But we're both going to need to be very careful."

Gage hoped he didn't regret this.

If he were honest with himself, he'd admit he was beginning to care about Nia more than he should. The woman was peacefully tenacious. Assertive without being abrasive. She stood for what was right.

But he hated thinking about her being in the line of fire, and he wasn't sure exactly what they would be getting themselves into.

Gage headed down the road, back toward the downtown area. They'd managed to get through most of the day without being chased. But he'd bet the men following them had eyes on Rob's apartment.

That meant he and Nia would need to plan their moves very carefully.

He was quiet for most of the drive, not wanting to say too much. He needed to think this through. He had to remain sharp and on guard. Failure could mean death.

Although . . . these people *did* want to keep Nia alive for some reason. That meant they probably wanted something from her. Something only she knew about or that she could do.

That either meant they wanted her money, her connections, or her knowledge.

Gage preferred that people didn't try to use Nia for anything.

After weaving through downtown, he pulled into a parking space near Rob's building.

He glanced at Nia one more time as he cut the engine. "You're sure you're up for this?"

She nodded, her gaze absent of any doubt. "I'm positive."

chapter
forty-nine

NIA TRIED to take a deep breath she and Gage stood outside of Rob's apartment. Danger seemed to crackle through the air. Anticipation seized her muscles.

This was it.

The moment they'd find out if their investigation would move forward or if it stalled.

They had no time for it to stall.

Not with Sophia being abducted.

Hot tears pressed at her eyes at the thought.

Gage punched in the code, and the lock turned.

As soon as she stepped inside, the memories hit her. Memories of waking up and seeing Rob's bloody body lying mere feet from her.

Her throat tightened as panic swirled inside her.

The moment had been so horrible. Something she'd never forget.

What she'd done afterwards hadn't been smart. Maybe she shouldn't have run.

But knowing Mario, she would be behind bars right now if the police knew she'd been here.

"Hey." Gage gripped her elbow, his eyes peering into hers. "Are you okay?"

Nia forced herself to nod. "Just lots of bad memories being here."

"I can imagine. But we need to keep moving. Okay?"

She nodded and followed Gage as he strode through the living room into a room she could only assume was Rob's bedroom.

He didn't bother to flip on the lights. Instead, he used the light on his phone.

It was better that way. Just in case somebody was watching.

He reached for her hand and pulled her toward another door in the distance.

The closet.

If Cormac was right, this was where the safe room was.

Another thought hit her, and Nia put on brakes. "You don't think Cormac is setting us up, do you?"

"I don't think so. Why would he do that?"

"I don't know what to think anymore."

"I'll open the door and step into the room first, just to be sure it's safe, okay?"

She nodded.

But as he started to step forward, Nia kept a grip on his hand and stopped him from going inside.

He turned back to her, confusion in his gaze.

Nia licked her lips, unsure of exactly what she wanted

to say. But the words were on the tip of her tongue. Words that showed how much she'd begun to care about him.

Something passed through Gage's gaze, and he nodded as if to acknowledge her worry and concern. To acknowledge that there was something growing between them. To acknowledge that, if he got hurt, they'd never be able to explore their feelings toward each other.

Then he let go of her hand and pushed Rob's clothes aside.

Gage swallowed hard, trying to forget the look in Nia's eyes and focus on the task at hand.

He spotted a panel at the back of the closet, one that blended in nicely with the woodwork. He used his thumb to slide the panel up.

A keypad appeared.

So far what Cormac had told them was correct. Gage prayed Nia was wrong and that Cormac wasn't trying in some way to set them up.

His jaw remained tight as he punched in the code and waited.

Two seconds later, he heard a click.

The code had worked.

A handle emerged from the wall.

Gage gripped it and slowly opened the door.

His throat suddenly went dry. This was it. The moment he could discover what all this was really about.

He shone his light along the wall and saw a switch. He flipped it, knowing that any light in this room would be concealed.

A small office came into view.

A desk stretched against the back wall with three computer monitors. A wood-topped table in the center of this space contained various handheld devices like phones and tablets. There were also wires, a headset, and some SIM cards.

Against the left wall was what appeared to be a drafting table that had been turned flat. Papers were scattered across it.

"It looks like a mad scientist worked in here," Nia murmured as she scanned the place.

"It does. This must be where Rob escaped when he needed some privacy. He was always paranoid people would steal his ideas."

"Intellectual property is something creators hold close to their vest. I can understand how he was protective of his ideas."

"So what exactly was he working on here?" Gage paced the perimeter of the small room. "Was it something that got him killed?"

Nia stepped farther inside and did another visual sweep of the place. "Good question. I'm not sure. I did mention something to him about his next project. I asked him when it might be ready so we could help him with the distribution of it."

"What did he say?" Gage studied Nia's face.

"He said he was working on something he thought had potential."

"What if that potential idea is what this is all about? I know Rob made millions with the Water Splat game. And I know he was excited about this new relaxation app he'd developed. If someone thought Rob had an idea for the next biggest thing, it might be worth killing over. But maybe they didn't anticipate the security measures he'd put in place."

Nia rubbed her arms and frowned. "I think you're right. It very well could have something to do with these apps he's been developing. If someone saw a payday . . ."

The two of them exchanged a look, knowing they were on to something.

Then Gage heard a click.

He froze.

He wasn't hearing things, he realized. His senses were trained to pick up on these things.

Someone else was in this apartment with them.

chapter fifty

NIA'S BREATH CAUGHT. Gage had heard it too. The sound.

Before she could react, Gage quickly shut the closet door, shoved the clothes back in place, and slid the safe room door shut.

The mechanism engaged with a churn, making it clear the lock had engaged. But Gage didn't look so confident. He leaned closer to the lock, his eyes narrowed.

"What is it?" Nia murmured, wondering what had him concerned.

"Usually, there's something on the inside of these safe rooms that disables the external lock."

"This one doesn't have it?"

He studied it more closely. "It doesn't look like it. I'm not sure if this is an older design or if Rob was in the process of replacing it or what. But it's not here."

"So that means if these guys have the code to get into

the room then they can?" Her throat tightened as she said the words.

They exchanged a look.

What did they do now? Just stand here and wait? If so, for how long?

"This was originally a safe room." Gage muttered, seeming to think out loud. He walked to one of the computers. "A lot of times, safe rooms are set up with cameras that show what's going on in other parts of the house."

"You think Rob set up cameras?"

"I think it's a good possibility. With today's technology, they could be hidden, and no one would even know."

Just like the ones in her office, Nia mused.

He grabbed one of the mouses and wiggled it.

One of the screens lit.

Sure enough, it showed a collage of four different black-and-white videos.

Black-and-white videos that showcased various parts of the apartment.

Nia's heart beat harder.

This could be their saving grace.

She skirted around the table at the center of the space and stood close to Gage. They stared at the screen, and Gage pointed at one video feed in particular.

It showed a man wearing dark clothing creeping around the living room.

Her eyes zoomed in on the gun in his hands.

Did that guy know they were in here? Had he seen

them enter the apartment, and was he looking for them now?

Or was he looking for something else?

She couldn't be sure.

At least Gage was with her. He had a gun. If it came down to it, maybe they stood a fighting chance.

Then another man appeared on screen.

Two intruders were in the apartment.

Nia watched as they explored the apartment.

Then they disappeared off the screen.

Nia's gaze flickered to a different area of footage.

That was when she realized the men had gone into Rob's bedroom.

Gage couldn't take his eyes from the security videos. He needed to know what those guys were going to do next.

What if this was a setup? If Cormac had led them here and told them the code only to trap them?

His heart thrashed into his ribcage as he waited to see what would happen.

He fisted and unfisted his hands, preparing his muscles to act. To grab his gun if needed.

But for now, he would wait.

The two men crept around the bedroom.

They didn't walk right to the closet.

That could be a good indication.

Gage heard Nia standing beside him, her breaths coming in shallow gasps.

He touched her elbow again, wishing he could comfort her.

But he didn't want to offer false hope.

She glanced at him, not bothering to hide the fear in her eyes.

He didn't blame her for being scared. Two men with guns stood close, with only a door separating them. However, this safe room, even if discovered, should protect them.

The guys walked closer to the closet.

Nia's breaths became even more shallow.

Rob had a camera mounted somewhere over the closet. As the men got closer, their faces came into view.

"You recognize either of those guys?" Gage whispered to her.

Nia shook her head. "No. I don't remember ever seeing them before."

That probably meant they were hired help. That the person behind this had some money stashed away and could afford to hire people to do his dirty work.

As one of the men opened the closet door, Gage reached for his gun.

The safe room would keep them protected . . . but only if these men didn't know the combination to get inside.

chapter
fifty-one

NIA FELT the anxiety bubbling inside her.

She didn't know how this would turn out. She wanted to believe she was safe.

But ever since she'd woken with Rob lying dead beside her, safety felt like an illusion.

Instead, her gaze remained riveted to the camera.

One of the men stepped out of sight and into the closet.

Her heart thumped harder.

Would they discover the door? Try to get in?

She could hardly breathe. She waited to hear the lock on the door click. She imagined seeing the door opening.

Gage stood beside her with his gun drawn and ready to use, if necessary.

Thump. Thump. Thump. Nia's heart was so loud she felt certain Gage could hear it too.

Dear Lord. Help us. Protect us. Guide us. In every way imaginable, we need You.

She waited, but she still didn't hear the lock turn. Didn't see the door open.

She glanced back at the screens again.

A moment later, the man stepped out of the closet and continued roaming around the room with his cohort.

They didn't know about the safe room!

The air left her lungs, and her shoulders drooped with relief. Still, she knew she and Gage might not be out of the woods yet, so to speak. They still needed to wait to see what these guys were doing.

Were they here looking for Gage and Nia? Or were they looking for something else?

She didn't know.

The men left Rob's bedroom and went to search the guest bedroom.

Then they went into the bathroom. Back down the hall. Into the living room again. Looked around in the kitchen.

After a few minutes, the men looked at each other and shook their heads.

They hadn't found what they were looking for.

They walked back to the front door, put their guns just out of sight, and left. The sight almost felt too good to be true.

Maybe she and Gage were safe . . . at least for a moment.

~

Gage wanted to feel relief, but he wasn't quite there yet.

What had those guys been looking for? Information on the cyber key?

He had no idea. But Gage would need to remain on guard just in case the men had left any "presents" for him and Nia in the apartment.

He didn't think that that was the case, but he couldn't afford not to explore every possibility.

Nia turned to him, the relief in her gaze obvious. "I thought we were goners."

He didn't want to admit it, but he'd feared the worst-case scenario as well. "We're still here."

She rubbed her throat and dragged in a shaky breath. "So what do we do now?"

"I think we need to look around the space and see if we can get any kind of idea of what Rob might have been working on. We need to figure out if he truly did have a secret project, and if that's what this murder and manhunt have been about."

"Good idea. I can start with his computer if you want to look over some of these papers on the drafting table."

"Sounds like a plan."

Gage began to rifle through the papers on the table, hoping to find something that might provide them with some answers. But much of what he saw was coding. There were a few hand-drawn diagrams. A graphic that maybe Rob wanted to use for a new app.

But most of it didn't make any sense to Gage.

He hoped Nia was having more luck.

She searched the files on the computer for several minutes before sighing and turning toward the table in the middle of the room. "There's nothing there—not that I can find."

"That's too bad, to say the least."

"Most definitely." She picked up one of the hand-held electronic devices there, hit a button on the screen, and frowned.

"You think the answers are on that?" Gage turned toward her, needing to clear his head a moment.

"At this point, I'm not sure of anything. What was the code to get into this room again?"

He told her the number combination.

She typed it into the tablet, and then her eyes widened. "I can't believe it. It worked."

She glanced at the screen when all of a sudden her face stilled, and it looked as if she was transported into another world.

chapter
fifty-two

NIA'S MIND reeled back in time.

Suddenly, she was laughing with Rob. Standing outside his apartment door.

She wasn't sure why she was going inside. The two of them were just having friendly banter, almost as if the tense discussion at dinner hadn't happened.

He unlocked the door, and they stepped inside.

Nia commented on how nice his place looked.

Rob set his keys on the entry table and then stepped farther inside, offering her something to drink.

She declined. Instead, she followed him into the living room.

As she paused near the couch, a man stepped from around the corner behind her.

Fear clutched her.

She couldn't see his face. She only felt the knife pressed into her back. Only saw Rob's face go pale.

"So glad to see that you guys could come join me," the man muttered.

"You don't have to do this," Rob muttered. "Nia has nothing to do with this."

"You know what I want. All you have to do is give it to me."

"You and I both know I'm not going to do that." Rob shook his head, a tremble to his voice.

"I told you if you didn't there would be consequences." The intruder pressed the knife harder into her back, the blade on the brink of breaking through her clothing to her skin.

"You need to put the knife down." Rob patted the air with his hands as he tried to get the intruder to calm down.

Nia's mind raced. Did she recognize that voice?

She wasn't sure.

She wanted to react. Wanted to say something. To do something. To ask questions.

But she couldn't.

She was frozen where she was. Even her vocal cords seemed immobile.

"I need something that you have," the intruder said. "And you're going to give it to me."

"I'm never going to do that," Rob said. "Never."

"Nia?" A deep voice called to her, jostling her from the moment.

Yet, just as she was frozen in real life, she was also frozen in the memory.

"Nia," the voice said louder.

The sound tried to pull her back, but she wasn't ready to come. She wanted to see this man's face. To recognize him.

But the memory was still blank.

No matter how hard she tried to remember, she couldn't.

Someone shook her. "Nia!"

She blinked.

Her thoughts slammed back into the present.

She saw Gage standing in front of her, a wrinkle of worry on his brow.

"Are you okay?" He gripped her arms.

She started to say fine but stopped herself. "A memory came back."

"What?" His voice trailed with anticipation. "Do you remember what happened?"

"Not all of it." Not even enough of it to answer very many of her questions.

But if this memory came back then maybe more would too.

Gage listened as Nia recited what she remembered.

She'd been so close to recalling who the person might have been. Even if Gage hadn't snapped her from the thoughts, he wasn't sure she would have remembered more. Not based on what she'd said.

But now it was clear that someone had come into the apartment and wanted something. It still didn't make sense why Nia had come up here with Rob. The move didn't fit her personality or Rob's.

They could figure that out later.

Right now, Gage wondered if the answers were somewhere in this room.

The memory had hit Nia after she'd looked at that tablet. Was that a coincidence?

Gage looked at the screen, but he didn't see anything of note. Only a whole bunch of app icons.

He frowned. Maybe the tablet hadn't triggered anything.

His only hope was that with time, Nia's memories would come back. That the pieces would come together. That answers would be found.

But Nia's sister had been abducted. Time wasn't on their side right now.

He glanced around the space one more time.

What were they missing here in this room?

Whatever secrets Rob was hiding had to be here somewhere.

chapter
fifty-three

NIA'S HEART still beat in overtime.

Being here.

Being close to Gage.

Being given a glimpse into the memory of what had happened on the night Rob died.

It all felt like too much, yet not enough.

How would she find Sophia? What would those men do with her sister?

She glanced back at the computers on the desk. "You don't suppose those cameras record anything, do you?"

Gage shook his head. "I already thought about that. But they're strictly for monitoring unless you hit record. So they didn't pick up on what happened."

"That's what I figured. But I thought it was worth asking." Nia sighed and glanced around. "I feel like the answers are here. Like they could be staring me in the face, and I'm still not sure what they are."

"We may need to come back and revisit this place after we sort out our thoughts more. But I can't make sense of most of these notes Rob wrote or the coding. What can you tell me about developing apps?"

She pressed her lips together as she tried to recall that information from long untouched mental files. "Based on what I've learned, when someone is developing an app, they come up with the idea. Then they come up with the coding and the graphics. Sometimes they'll have someone help them with that part. But Rob didn't need to do that, which was a good thing. People are always afraid their idea will be stolen in the process. The truth is that ideas themselves can't be copyrighted, but the execution of the ideas can be."

"Keep going," Gage said.

"The important thing is to keep the source secure. That was one thing that Rob was very adamant about. Even though we were going to help distribute the app for him, Rob—in some ways—was a one-man show. He wanted to be the one who worked with the companies to put his app on various platforms. I guess he learned his lesson the hard way when it came to Water Splat. All the vultures came out trying to steal his ideas."

"I know a whole bunch of rip-off games similar to his came out afterward," Gage said. "I think it bothered him."

"Maybe, but none of them were as good as Rob's, so he could have felt good about that. Anyway, I suppose there are ways that someone could reverse engineer the coding of the app to figure out what makes it work. But by the time an app is released, if you were to do that, then it would be clear you were simply copying someone else's idea."

Gage crossed his arms as he thought through what she said. "So the idea that someone was trying to steal this about-to-be-released app seems far-fetched?"

Nia thought about it a moment before nodding. "Kind of. However . . . this new idea Rob was developing, his third project . . . maybe *that's* really what this is all about. I only wish there was a way we could figure that out."

Before Gage could respond, his phone rang. He glanced at the screen and grimaced.

"What is it?" Nia asked.

"It's Brittany."

Gage hesitated another moment before answering. He put his cell on speaker so Nia could also hear.

"Gage?" Brittany sounded breathless. "Is that you?"

"It is. Nia is here with me. Is everything okay?" She didn't sound okay.

"I don't know," she whispered. "I think somebody is following me. I don't know what to do."

Gage exchanged a look with Nia. Was this all some kind of ruse?

It wouldn't surprise him if it was. Brittany hadn't

proven herself to be someone who always told the truth. For that reason, he needed to answer with caution.

"Why do you think someone is following you?" he asked.

"Because every time I turn around, I see the same man behind me. Sometimes he ducks out of the way so I won't see him. But I sense that he's there. I know he is."

Her fear did sound genuine, and there was the possibility that she was in the line of fire now also. "Where are you right now, Brittany?"

"I got in a cab. I figured it was the safest thing to do. But for all I know, this guy could be following me right now." Her words came out faster and faster.

"Here's what you're going to do," Gage said. "There's a diner near Bayfront Park that stays open late. Mickey's. Have you seen it before?"

"I have."

"Go there and wait inside. There should be plenty of people so you should be safe. Get a table, and Nia and I will be there to meet you in fifteen minutes. Got it?"

"Oh . . . okay. If you can meet me there that would be great. Thank you."

"Keep the phone with you, and if you need anything in the meantime, call me, okay?"

"I will. But hurry."

Gage ended the call and glanced at Nia. Neither of them had to say anything to know what the other was thinking.

This could be a trap. Brittany could be exaggerating. Leading them right into danger.

Neither of them had any idea what they would be walking into right now.

But Brittany had earnestly sounded fearful.

For now, Gage's first order of business would be to get Nia out of Rob's apartment safely and undetected.

chapter
fifty-four

A RUSH of relief swept through Nia when she and Gage stepped into the diner. The place was fashionably old-timey, though nothing about it was truly hometown, especially not the prices.

The scent of bacon and toast temporarily filled her with comfort.

But the emotion quickly dissipated.

Nia feared they'd run into those men again or that someone would find them. But so far, so good.

Now they needed to get through this meeting with Brittany.

She spotted the woman sitting in the corner with a cup of coffee in front of her. Her eyes were red as if she'd been crying.

A pang of compassion echoed in Nia's chest.

The woman looked truly upset.

But Nia reminded herself to remain cautious. The stakes were too high for her to let down her guard.

She and Gage slid into the booth across from Brittany.

Brittany sniffled before saying, "Thanks so much for coming."

"Glad you got here okay," Gage started. "Have you seen the man anymore?"

Brittany shook her head, strands of blonde catching in her tears and sticking to her cheeks. She raked her hair back, away from her face. "I thought for sure I was going to end up like Rob."

"Why don't you tell us what's really going on, Brittany?" Gage began. "We all know there's more to the story than what you've told us."

She glanced at a napkin in her hands, one she'd been using to wipe away her tears. She played with the edge, making little rips around the perimeter.

"None of this was my idea," she said, her voice cracking.

"What do you mean?" Nia's voice hardened. Brittany's words indicated she knew something more than she'd let on.

The fact didn't surprise Nia—but it did cause her distrust to harden even more.

"I mean, I was at Avenue 12 one night, and Darius and I got into a huge fight. We kind of broke up. I was walking to my car when I heard someone behind me. But before I could turn and see this person's face, I felt a gun against my back."

Nia hadn't expected that turn of events. "What happened next?"

"This guy told me not to look at him. Then he led me to a dark alley. I didn't know what he was going to do . . ."

More tears flowed from her eyes.

They waited for her to continue, to compose herself.

"He told me he knew how to get back at Darius for the way he'd treated me. Said I could make it work to my advantage." Brittany sniffled again. "He told me there was this guy, and I was just his type. Said I should hit on him, get him to like me."

"And this guy was Rob?" Gage's voice retained an edge of caution.

Brittany nodded, guilt filling her gaze. "He told me where Rob worked, and I 'accidentally' ran into him. I'm good at getting guys to like me, so I knew exactly what to do. Act a little bit like an airhead. Act like he was a hero. The setup worked like it always does, and Rob asked me out. We went on a few dates over the next couple of weeks."

Nia leaned closer, wanting to see Brittany's eyes when she asked the question. "Why did this man want you to do that?"

Brittany's expression crumbled again, and tears flowed.

Nia could appreciate that she was upset. But they were also operating on a time crunch here.

She tried to wait. But her patience was waning.

And it seemed like everything this woman said was a lie, so Nia wasn't inclined to believe everything Brittany told her now either.

Gage felt immune to the woman's tears.

It wasn't that he didn't feel sorry for Brittany. Part of him did. But he thought part of Brittany's act right now was purely histrionics.

"This guy said that going out with Rob would make Darius jealous." She sniffled again. "Said he'd possibly run back into my arms."

"And?" Nia asked. "Certainly, there's more to the story than that."

"He wanted me to find out some information from Rob," Brittany continued. "Something about some of those apps he develops. But the thing is, I don't know anything about technology. This guy said the information was somewhere at Rob's apartment, and all I had to do was find it."

"Did you find it?" Gage's spine tightened at the thought of his friend being taken advantage of.

Brittany shook her head. "I looked. I really did. Every time I got the chance. But I didn't find it. One time I tried to ask Rob about it, but he made it sound like he had no idea what I was talking about. I could tell he was starting to lose interest in me. Honestly, we didn't have much in common. I scrambled to figure out what to do. I got the sense the guy with the gun was serious. He said he knew where I lived. I just knew he was going to kill me if I didn't find what he wanted."

"You never saw his face?" Nia asked.

"I never saw his face. I promise. He was very secretive,

and I couldn't really tell much about him at all." Brittany shrugged. "I'm sorry I can't be of more help."

"What about the shooting at the club?" Gage started. "Did you have anything to do with that?"

She hesitated just long enough to make it clear she *did* know more than she wanted to share. "I think I might know what's going on—"

But before she could finish, gunfire erupted.

The windows beside them shattered. Screams filled the air.

"Everyone, get down!" Gage yelled.

Then he threw himself over Nia, covering her as glass rained around them.

chapter
fifty-five

GAGE GLANCED down at Nia as she lay beneath him on the bench seat of the booth. Her arms covered her head, and glass decorated her hair. Otherwise, she appeared unharmed.

"Are you okay?" he rushed.

Nia blinked several times before nodding. "Yes . . . I think so. I think I'm okay."

Tires squealed outside.

Then a moment of silence passed.

He finally raised his head again.

The gunman was gone.

Sirens already sounded in the distance.

They should be out of danger.

Gage rose, shaking off some stray shards of glass.

Then he glanced across the table to where Brittany was seated. He needed to make sure she was okay also.

But one look at her slouched body, and he knew she wasn't.

Blood bloomed on the pink, short-sleeved shirt she wore, and her eyes appeared still and lifeless.

Nia raised her head, and her gaze went to Brittany. "No . . ."

Gage rose and put a finger to Brittany's neck just in case. But his fears were confirmed.

The woman was dead.

Had someone targeted her just because they were afraid she would talk too much?

There was a good chance that was true.

He glanced around the rest of the room. Everyone else seemed shaken but okay.

Those guys had either followed Brittany or Gage and Nia. But he'd put his bets on Brittany.

But now these guys might fear what Brittany had told them.

They might try to get to Nia and himself next.

He grabbed her hand. "We need to get out of here."

She glanced outside as blue lights flashed in the distance. "But shouldn't we stay until the police—"

"It's not safe," Gage told her. "Those guys could come back. They might shoot us next time."

Her eyes widened with fear, but she nodded.

Gage tugged her toward the back of the building.

They'd deal with this mess later. No doubt there were security cameras. Someone might be able to identify them. The police would want to chat, to see if they had any involvement.

But right now, staying alive was more important.

Gage rushed out a back door and into a dark alley.

Holding Nia's hand, he ran down the alley toward the street.

They reached the sidewalk, but it was more crowded than he'd expected. People had stopped to stare after what had just happened.

Making a split-second decision, Gage ran in the opposite direction with Nia.

His gut told him there was more to come. That these gunmen would be looking for them.

As they reached another street, a car squealed nearby.

"Gage?" Nia sounded breathless.

"We've got to run faster."

There was no time to get back to their car. Besides, by now first responders had probably surrounded it.

"Where are we going to go?" Nia asked between gasps of breath.

That was an excellent question.

But the best thing they could do right now was to keep moving.

Movement is life, Gage mused.

So whatever they did, they couldn't stop.

Fear pulsed through Nia.

She couldn't get Brittany out of her mind. The blood on her chest. The lifeless look in her eyes.

How could someone have done this?

How could they have killed Rob?

Why were people so evil?

She wasn't naive. But she never wanted to become accustomed to the horrors taking place around her either, to think those things were normal.

Gage pulled her beside another building, and they ran as fast as they could.

Nia glanced behind her as she heard a car approaching.

The car pulled up beside them.

Another barrage of bullets flew toward them. The shots nicked the asphalt at their feet.

But they hadn't been hit. Not yet.

Did these guys want her dead after all?

"This way!" Gage pulled her down another alley and around a corner.

They continued to weave between buildings.

Would they really lose the gunmen this way?

Nia would have to rely on Gage's expertise on the matter.

The next alley they ran down ended at a brick wall, and Gage muttered beneath his breath.

Then they turned and glanced at the street.

A car appeared there.

It was them. Nia was certain of it.

"We've got to move!" Gage jerked her back toward the street—toward the gunmen.

What was he doing?

He paused by a fire escape next to an old, condemned apartment building. It appeared as if construction had started on the place to revitalize it.

But right now, it looked like a death trap with its broken windows and graffiti painted on the brick walls.

Nia's eyes widened as she realized what they were about to do.

She'd only seen things like this on movies and TV shows. She never thought she would experience this in real life.

The staircase lowered with a loud clank. Then Gage pulled her up a flight of steps.

As they climbed, footsteps rushed toward them. Men grunted.

Another bullet flew, pinging on the metal fire escape.

Nia muffled a scream.

At the first platform, Gage turned to an old window and shoved at the pane.

To Nia's surprise, it opened.

They climbed into an old apartment that looked like it hadn't been touched in years—other than by hoodlums up to no good.

Beyond the shadows of the room, the building was dark.

Danger loomed both behind them and in front of them.

What were they going to do now?

Panic raced through her.

"Gage, please tell me you have a plan."

chapter
fifty-six

GAGE GLANCED AROUND. Then, on a whim, he pulled Nia toward a door in the same room they'd climbed into. He opened it.

A closet.

This would work.

He pushed her inside the musty space. Moved a few boxes. Positioned her behind them. As he closed the door, he moved in himself.

"Shouldn't we have run farther?" she whispered, her breath brushing his cheek.

"That's what they'll think we're going to do. That's why we're hiding here instead."

"Do you really think this is going to work?"

"I have some experience with these things," he told her quietly. "You're just going to have to trust me."

Gage hoped and prayed his idea paid off.

They didn't have time to talk anymore.

Voices sounded in the room.

Footsteps echoed on the wooden floors.

There were at least two men. Could they be the same two men who'd been in Rob's place earlier? Gage wasn't sure.

"Where'd they go?" one of them yelled.

"You go left, I'll go right," another man responded. "Find them! Who knows what that little tramp said."

Little tramp? Were they talking about Brittany?

Nia's fingers dug into his arm as she stood behind him, listening also.

Seconds later, their footsteps scattered away.

But he needed to be sure they were gone.

He couldn't risk much. Not with Nia with him.

As they stood there in the dark, he was all too aware of her presence. Of her hands clutching his arm. Of her shallow breathing. Of the subtle smell of lilacs wafting from her.

Where had the scent even come from? She didn't have her normal toiletries with her.

It didn't matter. He liked the fragrance.

But this wasn't the time to think about it.

After several minutes of silence, Nia whispered, "What now?"

"Just a couple more seconds." Gage needed to be sure that those guys were far away.

If he'd been in those men's shoes, he would have probably separated like they did. Covered more ground. Searched the second floor. Then gone to the other floors to search as well.

That was what Gage was banking on.

Finally, enough time had passed that he felt like they could move.

"You ready?" he whispered to Nia.

"I . . . think so. I mean, yes. I'm ready."

"Follow my lead. You're going to have to trust me."

"Okay." Nia's voice cracked. "I do."

Then Gage opened the closet door.

Nia didn't know what Gage was doing. But she really did feel as if she could trust him. So far, he'd kept her safe.

He opened the door and glanced around.

Then he pulled her back toward the window they'd entered the building through.

Smart thinking.

He led her outside. Paused on the platform. Glanced around.

Then he quietly led her to the bottom of the staircase.

Once they hit the ground, they darted from the alley and onto the street.

The gunmen's car was still parked at the entrance of the space.

With no one inside.

They ran in the opposite direction.

Nia's heart nearly pounded out of control as the sidewalk and buildings blurred past. All she could think about was finding safety.

They just needed to make it back to the hotel. She needed to recalculate. To think everything through.

To figure out who might be behind this.

She'd thought at first that maybe it was Darius or Brittany. But now Darius was seriously injured, if he was even still alive. And Brittany . . .

Nia shivered at the memory.

But Cormac truly seemed like a victim here as well.

Whoever was behind this had enough money to hire those men to come after them. And they knew about the technology business. Knew that Rob was developing an app.

So who could it be?

That was what they needed to figure out.

But, first, she and Gage needed to get out of sight.

chapter
fifty-seven

WHEN GAGE and Nia got back to the hotel, adrenaline continued to pump through them.

He and Nia had managed to do it. They'd lost those gunmen. And they'd found that information in Rob's apartment.

Maybe they could finally move forward.

And in the process, they could save Nia's sister.

They stepped into the hotel room, and Gage locked the door behind them. Then he scanned the living room area—just to be on the safe side.

It looked clear.

Austin must have already gone to sleep because he was nowhere to be seen.

Gage turned to Nia. It was only then he realized how close they were standing.

Close enough to see the flecks in her eyes. To see the stray curls bouncing in front of her face. To see the smoothness of her skin.

Gage's heart lurched into his throat.

Adrenaline?

Maybe. But he knew there was more to it than that.

It had been a long time since Gage had let himself feel anything for a woman. He hadn't intended on letting himself feel anything for Nia.

But the feelings were there, and they were undeniable.

He was deeply attracted to Nia on more than one level.

As she stared up at him, he couldn't help but think that she felt the same way.

"We did it." Satisfaction bubbled in her voice. "We got the information, and we got away from those men."

"We did. I think we could really be onto something."

They both paused as their gazes locked.

The next moment, their lips met in an explosive kiss.

They both had too much pent-up energy. Too many adrenaline rushes. Too many brushes with death.

All that emotion all came out in their kiss.

A passionate kiss Gage wished would never end. Even their heartbeats seemed to pound in sync as their lips explored each other's, as their arms drew each other closer. Warmth spread through him.

Finally, he pulled away.

Even though his lips still felt on fire. Even though heat ran through his veins. Even though his heart pumped out of control.

Nia shared an intimate smile before touching her lips and taking a step back.

"I . . ." Her voice trailed as if she didn't know what to say.

He understood exactly where she was coming from.

"Maybe we should just go to bed—each to our own beds," he clarified. "And we can talk about things again in the morning?"

A crinkle of amusement tugged at her lips. "Good idea."

"If you get any texts or if you need me for anything, I'll be on the couch."

"I should be fine. But thanks."

He stepped back and ran a hand through his hair. He felt so discombobulated that he hardly knew what to do with himself.

He paused near the couch and nodded at her. "Good night then."

Nia nodded back. "Good night."

Nia wanted to tell Gage that there was no way she would need anything from him tonight.

Because the last thing she needed was to let her guard down and wander out toward him in the living room.

The last thing she needed was another explosive kiss like that.

That had been surprising. And nice. *Really* nice.

Who was she kidding? It was more than nice.

It was something she wouldn't forget for a long time . . . if ever.

The kiss had been a nice oasis of delight in the middle of otherwise harrowing circumstances.

A moment of guilt washed through her. This seemed like a poor time to be enjoying herself. Especially considering everything that had happened. Considering Rob. Considering Brittany. Considering Sophia.

Her guilt deepened a moment. Yet she couldn't seem to keep all her warm and gushing feelings at bay either.

There was something about Gage that was different —different in a very good way.

She slipped into her bedroom, knowing she needed some time by herself to recover from that kiss.

She had no idea what it meant. What her and Gage's future would look like, especially considering that Gage didn't even live around here.

She still had so much more she needed to learn about him.

Yet hope persisted. It had sprung up quickly, like a poor rancher discovering a hearty well of oil.

She sat on the edge of the bed. She needed to look through all the information she'd gathered and see what she could figure out. See if she could figure out this cyber key.

The answers were there somewhere.

But the day's events now messed with her head. Really what she needed even more was to get some rest and to rethink this in the morning.

The countdown was on, and she needed to figure out what she'd tell these guys in order to get her sister back.

She pulled off her shoes, deciding just to sleep in a T-shirt. Then she curled under the covers, determined to get her racing thoughts under control so she could fall asleep.

But before her head even hit the pillow, her phone buzzed.

Something internal told her to ignore it. But she couldn't. What if it was about her sister?

She glanced at the screen and saw that it was that same unknown number those demands had come from.

But this time, the message was different.

It read:

He's not who you think he is.

Then a picture was attached. A picture of Gage with his gun to the back of a woman who had tears streaming down her face. The hard look on Gage's face made him seem like a different person . . . someone evil.

chapter
fifty-eight

GAGE WOKE up the next morning with a surprising spring in his step.

He hadn't been able to get that kiss out of his mind.

He knew it was foolish, yet he couldn't stop himself from dwelling on it.

With that one act, he was suddenly starting to imagine himself with a real life. One that didn't revolve around work and covert assignments. Instead, he pictured one where he actually felt happy.

No, not just happy. But full of joy and peace.

In every scenario that ran through his head, Nia was a part of it. Could the two of them possibly have a future together?

Maybe that was something they could figure out before he left this area.

And he wasn't leaving here until he had answers about Rob.

This morning, Gage hoped to review some of the items they'd taken from Rob's apartment last night.

Maybe the answers were there.

They had to figure out exactly what to do about Sophia before eleven.

He'd had Austin check, and the woman truly was missing. These guys must have grabbed Sophia. Thankfully, it appeared they were keeping her alive.

But he and Nia would need to plan their next steps carefully.

Gage showered and wandered back into the kitchen, searching for something to eat.

At seven, Nia emerged from her room, already dressed and appearing as if she'd been awake for a while. If Gage had to guess, she hadn't been able to sleep.

Gage's smile faltered as soon as he saw her tense expression.

Something had changed. But what?

Nia glanced at him before averting her gaze. Then she paused beside the breakfast bar. "Hey."

Gage moved, shifting to stand in front of her. More than anything, he wanted to take her into his arms again.

But he knew better.

Instead, he waited for her to say more, to explain her distant attitude.

After a moment, she looked up and drew in a deep breath before asking, "Anything new?"

He swallowed the lump in his throat. "No. I'm hoping we can work on some things this morning."

"We don't have much time." Her voice sounded strained.

"I know. If you bring me the information we took from Rob's, we can study it together. Two heads are better than one, right?"

Nia nodded, that far-off look still in her eyes. "That sounds like a plan."

She started to step away, to go to her room to retrieve it when he touched her arm.

She stiffened, and Gage dropped his hand, shoving it back into his pocket.

Something was definitely going on—though he had no idea what.

He studied her pinched expression before asking, "Is this about your sister? I know this has to be unnerving."

Nia's gaze wavered a moment before she nodded. "I'm worried about her."

But Gage knew Nia wasn't telling the whole truth. There was more to her frosty reception.

He wanted to ask questions. He wanted answers.

But she was right. They didn't have much time.

If they wanted to rescue Sophia, then they needed to spend the next several hours just focusing on that.

Gage shoved aside his emotions, just as he'd been trained to do.

But if he were honest, he would admit that the tension pulling across his chest wasn't just because of this case and Rob's death.

It was also because of Nia's sudden change of heart.

Nia hated to act so distant toward Gage.

But she couldn't get that photo out of her mind. She knew she should just ask him about it.

But memories of Mario and everything she'd been through with him filled her mind.

Mario hadn't been the person she'd thought he was. In the end, the man had broken her heart, and he'd nearly ruined her reputation. She didn't want to go through that again.

No, she'd be better off focusing on her investigation into Rob's death and finding her sister. She'd never forgive herself if something happened to Sophia, especially if she could have prevented it if not distracted with her own emotions.

Yet every time she looked at Gage, her throat tightened, and she had to remind herself of everything at hand.

She sat on the couch, papers in front of her, and studied the design for the app.

While she did that, Gage talked on the phone to his boss, and Austin continued trying to find the security footage he needed. It was a bigger task than Nia had realized to track down all the cameras and hack into the servers. But if he was able to do that, they might have more answers.

Answers were exactly what they needed.

As she sat there, a memory of last night hit her. A

memory of Brittany talking to them in the booth one moment and slouched over dead the next.

Nia's lungs tightened at the recollection.

Poor Brittany . . . and right as she'd been about to tell them something about who might be behind this.

Her mind continued to race. She had no doubt the authorities would track her and Gage down. Most likely, there were images of them at the diner with Brittany. As soon as Mario saw them, he'd recognize her.

The last thing Nia wanted was to have to explain herself to him.

Then there were her own memories that had surfaced last night. Memories about what had happened after she left that restaurant with Rob.

Her jaw tightened at the thought.

If she could just remember a little bit more . . .

But the only suspect who made sense to her right now, the only person she could see being guilty, was . . . Sigmund O'Neill, another tech broker who wanted the deal.

He had the most reason to want those plans from Rob.

But Nia hadn't seen the man recently. Had Sigmund simply hired people to do his dirty work while he himself sat in his office and watched?

Or was she totally off-base? Maybe Sigmund wasn't guilty.

What about Jeff? He had been poking around Melissa's desk.

The questions made her head pound.

Austin suddenly sat up straighter in the chair across from her. "I think I found something."

Gage and Nia crowded closer. He showed them on his computer some video footage of Rob's apartment building. The time stamp showed it was just after midnight.

Nia gasped in a breath.

Someone familiar strode inside the building.

Someone she'd just been considering.

Sigmund O'Neill.

Nia's heart beat harder. That couldn't be a coincidence.

Was Sigmund behind this?

It was looking more and more as if that was the case.

chapter
fifty-nine

GAGE SHOULDN'T BE SURPRISED that Sigmund was most likely the one behind this. The man had been a suspect in Gage's mind the whole time, but he'd had nothing to prove it.

Now they had this evidence. Sigmund had come into the building at midnight and left thirty minutes later—enough time to kill Rob and frame Nia for it.

Gage had already called the man's office. His secretary said he hadn't come in today.

He was tempted to swing by the man's home. Gage still might do that. But he couldn't show up without a plan.

"What are you thinking?" Nia moved back to her seat on the couch, but the concern on her face was still evident.

"We need to figure out a way to catch this guy—in a way that no one gets hurt." Rob, Darius, and Brittany had already been casualties.

"I agree." Nia glanced at the time on her phone. "We only have an hour and a half before I'm supposed to give these people the cyber key information they want—and I'm still not sure what that information is."

Gage nodded stiffly, hearing the mental clock ticking in his head. "I would call in backup, but there's not enough time."

A strange expression crossed Nia's gaze. But as quickly as it appeared it was gone.

Her phone buzzed, and she glanced at it. Her face went paler.

"What's going on?" Gage could tell by her expression that something was wrong.

"It's Mario," she told him. "He keeps calling, but I've ignored his calls. I don't feel like dealing with him."

"He's calling about what happened at the cafe yesterday, I assume."

She nodded. "I knew the police would want to question us. I knew our images had probably been caught on camera, and cops knew we fled the scene. We look suspicious."

Gage couldn't argue with that. "Has he left any messages?"

She nodded. "He sounds angry. Keeps telling me about how much trouble I'm going to be in and that there's nothing he can do to protect me—not that he would. His words not mine."

Gage's muscles tightened again, even though he wasn't surprised.

Nia glanced back up at him. "Should I answer? Should we just get this over with?"

"We can't do anything rash," Gage said. "Let's just take five minutes to think it through. Then we can come up with our plan of action."

Nia's thoughts continued to race as she sat on the couch. Austin had slipped out to grab some specialty coffee drinks for them at the shop downstairs. Gage still studied some of the files they'd grabbed from Rob's place.

But she was having trouble staying focused.

She wanted to do the right thing. The thing that would ensure her sister's safety.

She mentally shuffled through all the options.

She picked up Rob's notes again and scanned them.

What was she missing? There was a lot of information here to go through. How could she narrow it down?

Sophia's life was on the line, and the pressure of knowing that scrambled her thoughts instead of making her sharper.

Too much was at stake. There were too many unknowns.

Tension squeezed at her chest.

Nia stopped at one page she hadn't examined yet. It was an analysis of a test study of the app Rob had sent to a few psychologists so they could give feedback and offer an endorsement.

Part of what made his app more appealing to users

was the test results behind it.

Nia read through some of the notes and stopped at a section that had been flagged.

"Why are you making that face?" Gage asked.

"I'm not sure this is anything." She sat up straighter. "But it looks like something happened during the test run on this app that had Rob concerned."

"What is it?"

She squinted as she read the words. "It says, 'Cannot recommend. Could have adverse effects.'"

"What?" Gage quirked an eyebrow. "Really? Can I see the prototype for this app?"

"Sure. If you let me see the tablet, I think I should be able to pull it up."

He handed it to her, and Nia hit several buttons.

But before she could open the files, the device glitched.

She let out an irritated growl. "I'm going to need to reboot this."

"I'm going to grab a granola bar from my room. You want one?"

"That would be great."

Gage disappeared down the hallway, and Nia continued to play with the tablet. Finally, she got it working and got the app pulled up.

All at once, something snapped in her mind.

Nia stood, no longer in control of her own body.

Even though she was barefoot, she shuffled to the door, opened it, and quietly closed it behind her.

Then she walked down the hall.

chapter
sixty

GAGE APPEARED from his bedroom and glanced around the living area and kitchen.

Nia was no longer on the couch. Where would she have gone? Her room?

"Nia?" he called.

There was no answer.

A bad feeling crept its way up his spine.

"Everything okay?" Austin stepped back into the hotel room, three cups of coffee on a tray in his hands.

"I'm not sure." Gage stepped past him, headed toward Nia's room. He didn't bother to knock.

Because he knew she wouldn't be inside.

And she wasn't.

"She's not here," he muttered.

Austin grunted. "She couldn't have gotten but so far. She was just here."

"You're right." Gage shoved his gun into his waistband. Then he quickly grabbed the papers and tablet Nia

Christy Barritt

had been looking at. He thrust them into a backpack and slung it over his shoulder.

He and Austin took off from the hotel room.

Gage glanced up and down the hallway, but Nia wasn't there.

He started toward the elevator but realized it would take too long. Instead, he and Austin took the stairs.

Just as they reached the lobby, he looked through the glass windows facing the street.

Nia climbed into a cab. Before he could reach her, the cab door closed, and the driver took off.

Gage stood, his gaze trailing her. "What is she thinking?"

"I have no idea." Austin paused beside him, his hands on his hips. "Something clearly changed between the time you left her and now."

"Yes . . . kind of like what happened at the restaurant with Rob." His thoughts raced.

Gage hailed a taxi. As he waited, he kept an eye on Nia's cab.

She was heading in the direction of Rob's apartment.

Was that where she was going? Had she thought of something else to look for? Was she headed there to get more information?

Finally, a cab stopped, and Gage and Austin climbed inside.

"Follow that yellow taxi up ahead." Gage pointed at the vehicle a quarter of a mile in front of them.

The driver—a gruff-looking fortysomething man—

glanced over his shoulder before shrugging. "Whatever you say."

Then he took off in pursuit.

The traffic was heavier and slower than Gage would have liked.

He didn't take his eyes off the cab.

He couldn't lose Nia.

Because something was going on here . . . something that was more than met the eye.

Nia didn't know why she needed to go to Rob's apartment. She just knew she had to get there.

Maybe she'd find answers there.

You should have told Gage, a quiet voice said inside her head.

Yet the voice seemed distant.

Distant and unreachable.

Nia almost felt as if she wasn't in control of her own mind, and her mind controlled her actions. And her actions . . .

She wasn't sure exactly what she would do next.

What was going on?

Why did it feel as if Nia was looking at herself from afar, unable to control anything?

Yet she was helpless to fix it.

She spotted the building up ahead and told the driver to stop.

But she had no money. How was she going to pay this guy?

Even though she was cognitive of that fact, her emotions and anxiety seemed to be turned off.

She opened her door and stepped out, her bare feet hitting the asphalt.

Before she could walk away, the cab driver lowered the window and yelled, "Hey, lady. You need to pay up. I don't know where you think you're going."

A man stepped toward them. Thrust some money at the driver. Told him to stay put a minute.

Nia studied the guy.

He was one of the men who'd been in Rob's apartment when she and Gage had broken in and hid in the safe room.

Danger . . .

Yet she couldn't move.

"We figured it was just a matter of time before you came." The man reached for her arm. "I'm going to need you to come with me."

"Where to?" Nia asked, possessing no will to fight.

"You'll see." He led her back into the taxi. Climbed in beside her. Slammed the door.

Then they took off.

chapter
sixty-one

AS THE YELLOW cab with Nia inside wove through traffic, Gage's muscles tensed.

They were wasting time—time they didn't have.

"Keep an eye on that cab," he muttered to Austin.

"Sure thing."

Gage might as well make good use of his time. He glanced at the papers he'd brought with him.

Were the answers in here somewhere?

The last thing Nia had been doing before she walked out was looking at the app and studying the paperwork.

Had she realized something and gone to check it out?

No, she wouldn't have just left like that.

Then Gage read one line, and his heart sank. "Oh, no."

"What is it?" Austin asked.

"I think I know what's going on."

"Hold that thought." Austin pointed straight ahead.

"Nia got out, but then she got right back in the same cab with a man."

Gage recognized the guy from Rob's apartment.

He leaned forward. "You still need to stay on that cab's tail."

"What do you think I am?" The driver shot a look at him in the rearview mirror. "Your personal employee?"

Irritation pinched Gage's spine. "You know what? Pull over."

"What?" The driver looked back at him, his eyes widening. "If you think you're going to ride and run—"

"Pull over and stop the cab. Now."

"Okay, fine. Whatever you say." The driver jerked the wheel to the side and stopped near the curb.

Gage burst from the cab and jerked the driver's door open. "Scoot over."

"What?" Fear laced the man's voice. "You can't just—"

Gage pulled out his gun. "Sorry to have to do this, but we need to move a bit faster."

The guy raised his hands. "I'm not looking for trouble."

"Perfect. Then scoot over. Now."

The driver did as he asked.

Gage climbed into the driver's seat, pulled on his seatbelt, and pressed the accelerator. It was time to utilize his defensive driving skills.

Wasting no time, he steered off the road and onto the sidewalk.

"What are you doing?" The driver muttered curses under his breath. "You're going to get me fired."

Drivers around him laid on their horns.

Pedestrians jumped out of his way.

"Don't worry. I'll take full responsibility for whatever happens." Gage needed to catch up to Nia, and nothing would stop him.

Nia's cab driver stopped outside an old warehouse, just as the man beside her instructed.

The man with Nia got out and then grabbed her arm.

They walked inside the dark, dank building.

Part of Nia knew she should fight. Try to stop this guy.

But she didn't.

She couldn't. Her willpower had left her.

He led her toward a smaller room at the back of the building.

As soon as she walked inside, she saw her sister sitting in an old swivel office chair with her hands tied to the arms.

At once, Nia's consciousness seemed to return to her body with a jarring force. No longer did Nia feel as if she was watching herself from afar.

Where was she? How had she gotten here?

She blinked as she glanced around.

Then she focused on her sister.

Sophia.

She was here.

Alive.

And bound and gagged.

Nia rushed toward her sister, tears flowing down her face. "Did they hurt you? I've been doing everything in my power to get you back."

Her sister murmured against the rag around her mouth.

Nia started to untie her when another memory hit.

A memory of being in Rob's apartment.

Of an intruder demanding Rob give him the semantics for his new app.

Of Rob refusing.

Being stabbed.

And then someone turning toward her and demanding her help, her expertise.

Her lungs tightened until she could hardly breathe.

"I hate to break up this happy reunion," a familiar voice tore her from the memory.

Nia's breath caught as she turned to confirm who the person was.

It wasn't Sigmund O'Neill. Perhaps he'd just been planted outside Rob's place as a distraction. Perhaps he'd been manipulated too.

Because the real guy stood before her now.

With a gun in his hand and determination in his gaze.

chapter
sixty-two

GAGE SUCCESSFULLY MADE it through the traffic.

The police weren't chasing him . . . yet.

It was just a matter of time. That meant he needed to move even faster.

The cab Nia was in eased to a stop beside an old warehouse.

Instead of pulling in behind the vehicle—which would have been too obvious—Gage stopped on the side of the street a block away. He reached into his pocket, grabbed a fifty-dollar bill, and shoved it into the taxi driver's hand.

"Thank you for your cooperation," Gage muttered.

The man scowled. "As if I had a choice."

Gage didn't argue. "You should call the police. Send them here. The sooner, the better."

The driver stared at him as if he'd lost his mind. Gage couldn't blame him.

He didn't answer, but that would have to work for now.

He and Austin hurried toward the warehouse, careful to remain in the shadows.

"You want to tell me what's going on?" Austin asked when they were away from the taxi driver.

"There was a note in the files," Gage explained. "About the test subjects for Rob's app. One of the psychologists working on the study made a note that the test subjects seemed to go into a trance-like state after using one part of the relaxation app.

"Is that because you can sometimes seem like you're in a trance when you're relaxed?"

"I don't think so." Gage crept along the building. "I think something about that app puts people into a highly suggestive hypnotic state. That's why all these things have been happening."

"This whole time I was thinking it was a serum that made people lose their memories," Austin said. "But you're right. I can totally see that."

"I think when Nia opened the app at the restaurant that night, seeing it triggered something in her. I'm not sure what. But she fell into a trance-like state. People are vulnerable to suggestions in that mental state, and I think someone told her to go with Rob to his place."

"What about Rob? Wouldn't he have noticed Nia seemed off?"

"Not necessarily. My best guess is that he was put into a similar state."

"That's twisted," Austin said.

"Yes, it is."

They reached the door.

"What's your plan?" Austin braced himself on one side of the entry while Gage stood on the other.

"It's the worst kind of plan of all," Gage said. "It's the play it by ear plan. I have no idea what we're going to find inside. But whatever happens, Nia can't be hurt."

Nia stared at Graham as he stood in front of her, two armed cronies at his side.

"*You* were behind this the whole time?" she muttered, shaking her head with disgust.

"Right under your nose, and you didn't even see it." He smirked.

Nia stood her ground, careful to keep herself between Graham and her sister. "I don't understand. What changed so quickly?"

He shrugged, looking a little too confident that his scheme was going to work.

Not if Nia had anything to do with it.

"You know those test results that were sent to Rob?" Graham said. "Since I was helping to oversee the project, they were sent to me as well. When I saw the part about the app putting people in a trance-like state, I got curious. I have connections with people who would find that ability very useful, especially if we could slide it in under the guise of an innocent little relaxation app."

She mentally snapped a timeline in place. "So you

must have gotten those test results right after our meeting with Rob in the office . . ."

"I did," Graham said. "Rob had just climbed into his car to go home when I called him and told him about the results. He hadn't read them yet, and he sounded as if he didn't believe me. He said he wanted to check it out himself. But he didn't seem excited about the opportunity of developing this more. In fact, he got antsy. Wanted nothing to do with it. That's when I knew I would have to be clever in order to make this work."

"So Rob went back to his apartment and called Cormac to get his opinion. I have a feeling that when Cormac saw something on the app, he realized that the study's findings were correct. He was put into a trance-like state as well." More pieces fell into place.

Graham grinned again. "That's right. And I'm able to implement that state whenever I want, just by saying a few words. That's what I did to you that night at the restaurant. Ran into you guys. Showed you something I'd 'discovered' on the app. As soon as I had you in the right mental state, I gave you the keywords. Told you what to do. When to do it. Made sure you and Rob both would forget I was ever there. Would forget anything you did while hypnotized, actually."

"You manipulated the situation . . ." Nia murmured.

"That's right. I always knew you were smart." Condescension marred his words. "The same images that could make a person relax could also make them slip into a suggestable mental state. And I knew if I could add some type of directive during that time then I could make people do whatever I wanted."

"It sounds dangerous," Nia muttered.

"It can be," Graham agreed. "That's why I knew I needed to jump on this before too many people found out about it and shut it down."

"So Rob tested the results, saw they were correct. He knew how dangerous this would be in the wrong hands. That's when he called Gage to help him figure out how to handle this. He called me about the same time to see if we could cancel the contract."

"Which I knew we couldn't do. In fact, I called Rob back and asked him for the plans. I knew if I had the semantics of the app, that I could help develop something like that on my own. But Rob refused."

"Why didn't security cameras pick up on you being at Rob's place?" Nia's thoughts raced ahead as she tried to put the pieces together—and buy time.

"I went in the back way."

"But how did you get inside?"

Satisfaction gleamed in his eyes. "A few weeks ago, after one of our meetings, Rob took me to his apartment to get some paperwork we needed. When he entered his security code, I paid attention. I memorized the sequence of numbers."

Nia shook her head. Her company dealt in confidential information. What else had Graham been memorizing? "So, that's how you got in. Then what happened?"

"I crept in after you both. Tried to talk Rob into

giving me the information, but he refused. One thing led to another and . . . it didn't end well for him."

"But you left me alive," Nia murmured. "Deleted the security footage of me going into the building even."

"Some guys I hired helped with that." He nodded toward his cronies.

"Why did you leave me alive?"

"I knew with your tech expertise you'd be able to figure out that stupid cyber key. But you've proven to be more difficult than I anticipated."

"So you took it as far as to follow me. Shoot at me. Kidnap my sister." Nia shook her head. "All so you can get a payout?"

"A very nice payout." His eyes continued to gleam with smugness. "And, in my defense, I didn't want to kill you at first. Only to scare you."

"But those men shot at me on the street."

His eyes darkened. "I didn't authorize that. I told the men who want to buy this tech from me about what was going on. They wanted to scare you into submission. I told them to back off, that you were no good to me dead."

"And the photo you sent me of Gage. Where did you get that?" She tried to make sense of everything.

"These guys I'm working with . . . they know things. They seemed to know something about this guy you've been hanging out with. In fact, they almost seemed to have a vendetta against him. He must have made some enemies."

Her heart thundered harder in her chest as the reality of Gage's past career became clearer.

"When I saw you talking to Brittany, everything changed . . ." Graham continued. "That's when I realized you knew too much. You became a liability. And the fact that you refused to do what I'd asked . . ." He glared at her.

"I can't believe you'd do all this." The thought made nausea churn inside her.

"All I want is a nice house on the beach and endless hours to do whatever I want. You can't really blame me for that, can you? At the rate I'm going right now, I'll be forced to work at least another fifteen years. That just won't work for me."

Nia's neck stiffened as she stared at the very man she'd once hired to work at her company, the one she'd thought had potential. Who'd come highly recommended and full of accomplishment.

How could she have been so wrong?

She stared at Graham, not bothering to hide the disgust in her gaze. "It all sounds selfish, if you ask me."

"Well, I didn't ask you. Besides, you're not going to remember most of this conversation anyway." He held up a prototype of the app and hit a few buttons.

Nia knew what would happen next, and she pressed her eyes closed.

Was it even possible to stop herself from going into a trance-like state again?

She had no idea.

chapter
sixty-three

GAGE PAUSED outside the office door. He'd left Austin in the warehouse's shadows just in case he needed backup.

He peered inside and saw Graham holding up the tablet toward Nia.

She pressed her eyes shut.

"Open her eyes!" Graham told one of the men in the room with them.

Gage had no time to waste.

Gun in hand, he burst into the room. When he saw the man reaching for Nia, he did a roundhouse kick.

Gage's foot hit the tablet in Graham's hands, and it fell to the floor.

Nia's eyes flew open. "Gage!"

The man closest to Nia turned and raised his gun.

Before Gage could aim his own gun and pull the trigger, the second henchman jammed the butt of his gun into the side of Gage's head.

Pain split through him, and he doubled over.

Graham scowled. "Did you really think that would work?"

The first guy snatched Gage's gun and shoved it into his waistband. Then he raised his own gun at Gage again, his finger poised over the trigger.

"No!" Nia threw herself between the gun and Gage. "Tell him to stand down, Graham. He'd have to shoot me first, and I know you don't want that to happen. You need me."

"I do need those plans," Graham muttered with a sneer.

Nia patted the air with her palms as if trying to calm the situation. "Then let everyone else go. You just need me."

"I can't let this guy and your sister walk away." Graham let out a chuckle. "They know too much."

"But don't you see? You can let them go," Nia murmured. "You have the power to make them forget this. No one else needs to die."

"Nia . . ." Gage said behind her.

He couldn't let her do this. Couldn't let her sacrifice herself for him.

But that was exactly what she was planning.

"Move out of the way," Graham muttered. "I *will* order my guys to shoot—but just enough to make you hurt and not kill you."

Gage's throat tightened.

The next instant, he lunged forward and wrapped Nia in his arms.

He turned and dove to the ground just as gunfire split the air.

Nia nearly lost her breath as Gage threw them both to the concrete floor.

Then she froze as she heard bullets flying.

But no pain came.

No bullets hit her.

Had they hit Gage?

She didn't think so. The sound had come from a distance.

The warehouse maybe?

Graham muttered for his guys to go check things out. Then he turned to Nia and Gage, holding his own Glock. "Get up. Both of you."

Nia stared at the gun as she and Gage slowly climbed to their feet.

She knew what was about to transpire. She could feel it in her bones. Could feel as if she and Gage had some type of mental connection.

He had a plan.

She glanced at Gage. He stood with his hands in the air near the door, the picture of compliance.

More gunfire exploded in the distance. The sound thundered through her chest and spiked her anxiety until she could hardly breathe.

Nia prayed everyone was okay.

But the sound was just enough to distract Graham.

Gage swung his leg around. Hit the weapon. It went flying to the floor.

"Get the gun!" Gage yelled.

Nia dove for it while Gage subdued Graham. In two seconds flat, Gage had the man pinned, stomach to the floor and hands behind him.

Gage pulled some zip ties from his pocket—almost as if he carried them everywhere like most people carried their wallets—and secured the man's hands.

"I don't know what you think you're doing!" Graham yelled.

Gage looked at Nia, noting she seemed okay.

Thank goodness.

"Stay here," he told her. "Keep the gun on him, and don't let him make a move. I'm going to go check out things and make sure Austin is okay."

Nia nodded and lifted a prayer.

Then she watched Gage disappear.

chapter
sixty-four

GAGE RAN INTO THE WAREHOUSE. Saw two men sprawled on the floor.

Were either of them Austin?

His heart lodged in his throat as he searched for his friend.

Then movement in the shadows caught his eye.

Gage aimed his gun.

"It's just me." Austin strode from the shadows. "I got them both."

Relief washed through Gage.

He felt incredibly grateful now for all their training.

It appeared that most of the danger was over.

Until sirens sounded outside.

The next instant, several police officers flooded the space.

Good. They would arrest Graham, and the man would finally learn his lesson.

Gage's relief was only temporary.

Another man strode inside behind the uniformed cops.

Mario.

Gage's throat tightened.

The man glanced around, hands on his hips like he owned the place.

As his officers checked out the men lying on the floor, Mario walked straight to Gage.

The man observed him a moment before letting out a grunt.

"You do this?" Mario nodded toward the bodies.

Gage shrugged. "They were going to kill Nia."

"Sounds like you have a lot of explaining to do." His gaze hardened. "Where is she?"

Gage nodded toward the office. Even though Mario was a jerk, he didn't think the man would hurt Nia. Especially not in a place like this with so many people around.

But the guy could make her life more difficult.

Gage would fight with everything inside him to make sure that didn't happen.

Nia had peered out from the office. Had seen Gage was okay.

Relief flooded her. Praise God.

Then she watched as Mario stepped inside the office. As his officers apprehended Graham, she lowered the gun onto the table and began to untie her sister.

But she couldn't ignore the smug look on Mario's face.

"What have you gotten yourself into now?" he chided as he shook his head and let out a *tsk-tsk*.

"My friends and I brought down this man who has not only had at least two people killed but also who abducted my sister." She nodded to Sophia as she continued to untie her. "Graham was also planning on selling dangerous technology to some less than honorable people who wanted to use it to hurt others. You should be thanking me right now."

Surprise flickered in his gaze but quickly was replaced with vengeance. "You fled a crime scene last night."

"That's your biggest worry right now?" She shook her head in disgust. "I guess I shouldn't be surprised."

"There's a lot about me that might surprise you," he muttered.

Nia freed her sister's arms, and the two pulled each other into a hug.

Mario stared at them and let out a grunt before stepping back. "I'll have questions for both of you."

Nia and Sophia held on to each other. "Of course."

"Don't go anywhere."

He was in over his head, Nia realized. Not just with this case. But with his job. With the compromising situations he'd put himself in.

This man was no leader.

He was a bully.

He stepped out of the room to answer some questions from his guys.

She instantly relaxed as soon as he was gone.

This was over, Nia realized. There would still be a lot of questions. A lot of answers that she needed to give.

But Graham wouldn't hurt anyone else.

And Nia needed to destroy this app before it did any more harm than it already had.

chapter
sixty-five

FOUR HOURS LATER, Nia, Gage, and Austin were finally able to leave the police station. Sophia had been taken to the hospital to be checked out, but she would be fine. Doctors wanted to keep her overnight for observation, just in case.

Graham and his men were either being treated or were behind bars. All of them would live to see another day—and pay for what they'd done. Nia only hoped the police would be able to track down the potential buyer of the app, the people who wanted to use it for nefarious purposes.

"You guys, I'm going to go grab a coffee." Austin nodded to a coffee shop on the corner. "I'll meet you back at the hotel room in an hour or two."

Gage nodded. "Sounds good. See you there."

Gage and Nia strolled along the street, in no hurry to get anywhere. They had a lot to talk about—and a lot to process.

"Thank you for coming for me." Nia stole a glance at Gage.

"Of course I came for you."

"I got a glimpse of that app, and that must have been what did it. Suddenly, I couldn't think for myself. My body felt like it was on autopilot."

"Can you imagine what someone could do with that kind of power if it was in the wrong hands?" Gage shook his head as if disgusted by the idea.

"Thankfully, it won't be."

They paused on the corner and listened to a lone ukulele player strumming and singing "I'm Yours" on the other side of the street.

Nia's thoughts whirled as she tried to find the words to say. Where did she even start? Before she could, Gage spoke up.

"Why were you acting strange this morning?" Gage studied her face, searching for answers. "Was it because of the kiss?"

"Yes." She paused and shook her head, resignation pressing on her and tugging at her features. "I mean, no."

"Well, which is it?" He continued to study her face, confusion in his gaze.

Nia let out a soft breath as she tried to explain. "The truth is someone sent me a photo. Of you."

"Of me?" Confusion flashed in his eyes.

She licked her lips, which suddenly felt dry. "You had a gun, and you held it to a woman who looked terrified. The thing is, I thought I knew who Mario was, but I didn't. It's been my fear that will happen again. That I'll

be tricked and feel like a fool. So when I saw that photo . .
."

"I don't know who sent that or where they got it."

"Graham said the men who wanted to buy that app .
. . that they somehow had access to it. That they seemed
to know who you were."

A shadow flickered across his gaze. "Is that right?"

"You know who might have sent it?"

He offered a stiff shrug. "There are several people it
could have been. I'd need to narrow it down."

She nodded slowly. "I see."

There was so much she still didn't know about him.

"Can I see the photo?" he asked.

Nia nodded and found it on her phone. She watched
Gage's face as he stared at it. She wanted to see surprise.
To hear denial.

Instead, Gage looked off into the distance and
frowned. "That's a real photo."

"What?" The word came out in a rush of breath.

Gage nodded toward a park in the distance. "I know
you need to go visit your sister in a moment. But can we
sit down and talk for a minute?"

"Of course." Nia braced herself for whatever he had
to say.

Gage felt butterflies in his stomach.

And he *never* felt butterflies. Everyone told him he
had nerves of steel.

But not right now.

He led Nia to a bench facing the water, and they sat down.

It took him a moment to find the right words. There was so much he wanted to say. So much he couldn't say.

"That photo was from a top-secret assignment I did," he finally started. "I know the woman in the photo looked innocent, but she was actually married to a powerful terrorist leader."

"She looked so scared."

"She *was* scared. I didn't shoot her. We turned her, actually, and she began to give us information on her husband and his exploits. Because of that, some major attacks were thwarted. Innocent lives were saved. The photo looks violent, but there was so much more to it than that."

"I see." Nia nodded slowly as if still trying to comprehend everything.

"The truth is, there are a lot of assignments I did that I can only half remember," he continued. "As part of the experiments that were done on me, I was programmed to obey."

"So I guess you understand what it was like for me when I fell under the spell of that app."

Gage ran a hand through his hair, that familiar tug-of-war beginning inside him. The assignments he'd done had been important. Had helped keep people safe. But that was never as cut-and-dry as people would like to think.

Peace came at a price. Most people weren't willing to accept what that price was.

"Unfortunately, I do understand what it's like to be controlled," he finally said. "I understand all too well. It's unnerving, isn't it?"

"Definitely."

"I struggle with my job. I struggle with my time in the military. Most of my colleagues do."

Nia turned toward him. "Then why don't you get out of that type of work? Do something else?"

"Because the guys at The Shadow Agency . . . they understand me when no one else does. No one else can fully comprehend what we've been through. And I've had my doubts about if I can truly acclimate to civilian life."

"I get how that would be hard." Nia offered a soft smile. "But I also believe that all things are possible, especially when we have the right processes in place . . . and faith in God."

A smile feathered across his lips. "I agree. But change can be hard."

"Does this mean you're going back to . . . Wichita?" Her question ended with a dubious lilt.

Gage smiled again. "The company is actually based in Michigan. And, yes, I will need to go back there for a while. But I'm hoping to come back to Miami to visit . . . often."

Her breath caught. "Really?"

"Absolutely."

A grin stretched across her face. "I'd like that."

Their gazes locked. "I'm glad to hear that."

As Nia studied his face, she pushed a curl behind her ear and swallowed hard. "Thank you for trusting me with everything you just said, Gage. It means a lot."

"I'm not supposed to talk about these things."

"But you shared them with me?" Questions danced in her eyes.

"Only because I care about you. I know it sounds crazy. We haven't known each other that long. But it's true."

"It's not crazy to me. I care about you too."

Hope filled him, and Gage felt as if a weight had been lifted from his chest.

Maybe he could acclimate to regular life. Maybe he could have a normal future.

Maybe he would have the chance to find some happiness for himself after so many years of helping others.

Gage leaned toward Nia, and their lips met again in what he hoped would be one of many more kisses.

epilogue

Two weeks later

NIA WAS THRILLED that her sister was safely back home and doing as well as ever.

Even though Graham had been arrested, things had returned to normal at the office—other than Rob's app being canceled.

Initially, Nia had suspected Jeff might be behind some of this, but it turned out that the man just had a crush on Melissa and had been trying to build the courage to leave her a note on her desk. The two were going on their first date next weekend.

Sigmund O'Neill had also been cleared. He had nothing to do with any of this.

Darius was still recovering. The man had some connections with Graham's buyers and had been putting pressure on Graham. Graham decided to take care of that by implicating Cormac in the process.

The new project Rob had been working on was a shopping app and nothing nefarious or dangerous.

Only Graham was guilty—Graham and the men he'd hired. The police were still searching for those buyers. Nia didn't like the thought that they were still out there. But she prayed they'd be apprehended soon.

As Nia sat in her office, the phone rang. She recognized the number and answered, putting it on speaker.

"Ms. Anderson," District Attorney Jack Henson started. "I hope I'm not catching you at a bad time."

"Not at all. What can I do for you?"

"I wanted to let you know that we're moving forward with the charges against Police Chief Mario Cruz. We've reviewed all the evidence against him and believe he's broken the law on more than one occasion, and we've lost our confidence in him as police chief. There's a process we'll have to go through, of course. But as of now, he has been relieved of his duties."

Nia sucked in a breath. She'd known it was risky when she'd gone to the DA with that information. But she couldn't hold back on it anymore.

What Mario had done—and most likely was still doing—was wrong. His actions could put him in a compromising position.

"We'll probably need more statements from you in the future."

"Whatever I can do," Nia told him.

"Very good. We don't believe that Mario will retaliate against you. Besides, we have other witnesses who have come forward—including Darius. Some prostitutes and even a few friends have turned on Mario. So we have no reason to believe he'll target you. But if you feel you need personal protection or a bodyguard . . ."

"I think I'll be okay." Nia looked up as someone knocked on her door, and a smile spread across her face.

She would *definitely* be okay now—as long as Gage was keeping an eye on her.

She thanked the DA and got off the phone. Then she rose and hurried across her office toward Gage. As he shut the door behind him, Nia wrapped her arms around his neck, and he rested his hands at her waist.

"You're early," she murmured.

"I couldn't wait another second to see you again."

He'd left eight days ago for another assignment, but he'd promised to return on his days off to visit her. Now she had him to herself for the next five days.

"Did I hear something about you needing a bodyguard?"

"You did. I was hoping you might want to fill that position."

He grinned. "I'd be glad to."

He leaned down and pecked a quick kiss on her lips.

A kiss that left Nia wanting more.

But not now.

Instead, they stepped back, and Gage offered his hand. "You ready to go to lunch?"

"I would love to."

As they stepped out of her office, Nia couldn't help but reflect on how things turned out.

Rob and Brittany were dead, but Darius was expected to make a full recovery.

Her sister had been put through trauma. But she was safe now.

And that app had been kept out of the hands of men who'd like to use it for their own advantage.

Men like Graham. Men who operated in the shadows.

But not everyone who did things out of the limelight did it for nefarious reasons.

She squeezed Gage's hand harder.

There were still good people out there. People like Gage.

And that was something Nia would always appreciate.

He got up, rebuked the wind, and said to the waves, "Quiet! Be still!" Then the wind died down and it was completely calm.

She remembered the verse on the picture near her door. That was what she wanted. To rebuke evil. To trust God. To find the calm through Him.

All as she walked through life with Gage at her side.

Thank you so much for reading ***Shadow Operative***. If you enjoyed this book, please consider leaving a review.

Stay tuned for ***Shadow Chaser***, coming next!

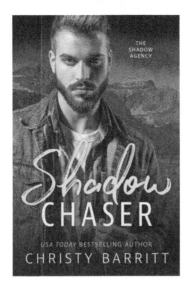

also by christy barritt:

you also might enjoy:

LANTERN BEACH BLACKOUT

Dark Water

Colton Locke can't forget the black op that went terribly wrong. Desperate for a new start, he moves to Lantern Beach, North Carolina, and forms Blackout, a private security firm. Despite his hero status, he can't erase the mistakes he's made. For the past year, Elise Oliver hasn't been able to shake the feeling that there's more to her husband's death than she was told. When she finds a hidden box of his personal possessions, more questions—and suspicions—arise. The only person she trusts to help her is her husband's best friend, Colton Locke. Someone wants Elise dead. Is it because she knows too much? Or is it to keep her from finding the truth? The Blackout team must uncover dark secrets hiding beneath seemingly still waters. But those very secrets might just tear the team apart.

Safe Harbor

Guilt over past mistakes haunts former Navy SEAL Dez Rodriguez. When he's asked to guard a pop star during a music festival on Lantern Beach, he's all set for what he hopes is a breezy assignment. Bree hasn't found fame to be nearly as fulfilling as she dreamed. Instead, she's more like a carefully crafted character living out a pre-scripted story. When a stalker's threats become deadly, her life—and career—are turned upside down. From the start, Bree sees her temporary bodyguard as a player, and Dez sees Bree as a spoiled rich girl. But when they're thrown together in a fight for survival, both must learn to trust. Can Dez protect Bree—and his carefully guarded heart? Or will their safe harbor ultimately become their death trap?

Ripple Effect

Griff McIntyre never expected his ex-wife and three-year-old daughter to come to Lantern Beach. After an abduction attempt, they're desperate for safety. Now Griff's not letting either of them out of his sight. Bethany knows Griff is the only one who can protect them, despite the fact that he broke her heart. But she'll do anything to keep her daughter safe—even if it means playing nicely with a man she can't stand. As peril ripples through their lives, Griff and Bethany must work together to protect their daughter. But an unseen enemy wants something from them . . . and will stop at nothing to get it. When disaster strikes, can Griff keep his family safe? Or will past mistakes bring the ultimate failure?

Rising Tide

Benjamin James knows there's a traitor within his former command. The rest of his team might even think it's him. As danger closes in, he must clear himself and stop a deadly plot by a dangerous terrorist group. All CJ Compton wanted was a new start after her career ended under suspicion. Working as the house manager for private security group Blackout seems perfect. But there's more trouble here than what she left behind. As the tide rushes in, the stakes continue to rise. If the Blackout team fails, it's not just Lantern Beach at stake—it's the whole country. Can Benjamin and CJ overcome their differences and work together to find the truth?

LANTERN BEACH BLACKOUT: THE NEW RECRUITS

Rocco

Former Navy SEAL and new Blackout recruit Rocco Foster is on a simple in and out mission. But the operation turns complicated when an unsuspecting woman wanders into the line of fire. Peyton Ellison's life mission is to sprinkle happiness on those around her. When a cupcake delivery turns into a fight for survival, she must trust her rescuer—a handsome stranger—to keep her safe. Rocco is determined to figure out why someone is targeting Peyton. First, he must keep the intriguing woman safe and earn her trust. But threats continue to pummel them as incriminating evidence emerges and pits them against each other. With time running out, the two must set aside both their growing attraction and their doubts about each other in order to work together. But the perilous facts they discover leave them wondering what exactly the truth is . . . and if the truth can be trusted.

Axel

Women are missing. Private security firm Blackout must find them before another victim disappears. Axel Hendrix likes to live on the edge. That's why being a Navy SEAL suited him so well. But after his last mission, he cut his losses and joined Blackout instead. His team's latest case involves an undercover investigation on Lantern Beach. Olivia Rollins came to the island to escape her problems—and danger. When trouble from her past shows up in town, she impulsively blurts she's engaged to Axel, the womanizing man she's seen while waitressing. Now, she may not be the only one in danger. So could Axel. Axel knows Olivia might be his chance to find answers and that acting like her fiancé is the perfect cover for his latest assignment. But he doesn't like throwing Olivia into the middle of such a dangerous situation. Nor is he comfortable with the feelings she stirs inside him. With Olivia's life—as well as both their hearts—on the line, Axel must uncover the truth and stop an evil plan before more lives are destroyed.

Beckett

When the daughter of a federal judge is abducted, private security firm Blackout must find her. Psychologist

Samantha Reynolds doesn't know why someone is targeting her. Even after a risky mission to save her, danger still lingers. She's determined to use her insights into the human mind to help decode the deadly clues being left in the wake of her rescue. Former Navy SEAL Beckett Jones needs to figure out who's responsible for the crimes hounding Sami. He's not sure why he's so protective of the woman he rescued, but he'll do anything to keep her safe—even if it means risking his heart. As the body count rises, there's no room for error. Beckett and Sami must both tear down the careful walls they've built around themselves in order to survive. If they don't figure out who's responsible, the madman will continue his death spree . . . and one of them might be next.

Gabe

When former Navy SEAL and current Blackout operative Gabe Michaels is almost killed in a hit-and-run, the aftermath completely upends his life. He's no longer safe—and he's not the only one. Dr. Autumn Spenser came to Lantern Beach to start fresh. But while treating Gabe after his accident, she senses there's more to what happened to him than meets the eye. When she digs deeper into his past, she never expects to be drawn into a deadly dilemma. Gabe has been infatuated with the pretty doctor since the day they met. Now, can he keep her from harm? Could someone out of his league ever return his feelings or will her past hurts keep them apart? As danger continues to pummel them, Gabe and

Autumn are thrown together in a quest to find answers. More important than their growing attraction, they must stay alive long enough to stop the person desperate to destroy them.

LANTERN BEACH BLACKOUT: DANGER RISING

Brandon

Physically he's protecting her. But emotionally she's never felt more exposed. The last person tech heiress Finley Cooper ever wanted to see again was Brandon Hale. Two years ago, Brandon shattered her heart. Now Finley needs protection, and, against her wishes, Brandon is assigned the job. Even worse, they must pretend to be a couple in order to find answers. Brandon, a former Navy SEAL, met Finley while on an undercover assignment in Ecuador. But he broke her trust, and now he doesn't blame Finley for hating him. As a new Blackout operative, Brandon's first assignment throws him into Finley's life 24/7. Someone wants her dead, and it's clear this person won't stop until that mission is accomplished. To keep her safe, Brandon must regain Finley's trust. Can he convince her she's more than a job to him? Or will peril permanently silence them?

Dylan

His job is to protect her. The trouble is . . . she doesn't want protection. Former Navy SEAL Dylan Granger's new assignment requires him to use both his tactical abilities and his acting skills. Hired by Katie Logan's father, his job is to protect the gutsy university professor while concealing his identity. To maintain his cover, he takes the unassuming role of her new assistant. Katie—a disgraced reporter—has stumbled upon a lead she can't ignore. Now it's clear someone is targeting her, but she refuses to back down. Her handsome new assistant is a welcome distraction from the chaos. But Dylan's skillset goes way beyond his job description, and Katie begins to suspect there's more to Dylan than he's letting on. Dylan's mission can't be disclosed—not if he wants to keep Katie safe. But as his feelings for her grow and the danger increases, keeping his secret becomes more of a challenge than he ever imagined. With innocent lives on the line, Dylan must choose between protecting Katie or savings others.

Maddox

He's on the case . . . and she's his prime suspect. Classified technology is missing, a delivery driver is dead, and former Navy SEAL Maddox King must find the culprits before a dangerous plan is enacted. To find answers, the Blackout agent must go undercover as a maintenance man at millionaire Seymore Whitlock's estate. While there, he sets his sights on Whitlock's personal assistant, Taryn Parsons, a woman who has everything to gain and nothing to lose. Six months ago, Whitlock plucked Taryn out of obscurity to become his caretaker. But with deadly incidents haunting the estate, Taryn doesn't know who she can trust—including the new maintenance man who is both intriguing . . . and unnerving. The stakes continue to escalate, and Maddox is running out of time to find answers. With the body count rising along with his list of suspects, this assignment may be his most challenging yet . . . for both his skillset and his heart.

Titus

She shattered his heart once. Can he set her betrayal aside for the sake of his country? The last person Titus Armstrong wants to join forces with is the woman who dumped him for his brother, Alex. But Presley Lennox is Blackout's best chance at infiltrating a dangerous organization known as The System and finding out more about their deadly plans. Presley Lennox wants out—of both an abusive relationship and the radical group she's become entangled with because of Alex. When Titus reappears in her life, he's like an answer to prayer—until he asks her to dive deeper into the very life she's been trying to escape. A dangerous plan is brewing that could destroy thousands of lives. Titus and Presley may be the only ones who can stop what's about to be unleashed. Failure would mean certain chaos . . . not only for them but for their nation.

about the author

USA Today has called Christy Barritt's books "scary, funny, passionate, and quirky."

Christy writes both mystery and romantic suspense novels that are clean with underlying messages of faith. Her books have sold more than three million copies and have won the Daphne du Maurier Award for Excellence in Suspense and Mystery, have been twice nominated for the Romantic Times Reviewers' Choice Award, and have finaled for both a Carol Award and Foreword Magazine's Book of the Year.

She is married to her Prince Charming, a man who thinks she's hilarious—but only when she's not trying to be. Christy is a self-proclaimed klutz, an avid music lover who's known for spontaneously bursting into song, and a road trip aficionado.

When she's not working or spending time with her family, she enjoys singing, playing the guitar, and exploring small, unsuspecting towns where people have no idea how accident-prone she is.

Find Christy online at:
www.christybarritt.com
www.facebook.com/christybarritt
www.twitter.com/cbarritt

Sign up for Christy's newsletter to get information on all of her latest releases here: **www.christybarritt.com/ newsletter-sign-up/**

 facebook.com/AuthorChristyBarritt

 x.com/christybarritt

 instagram.com/cebarritt